The Kaiser's Butterfly
Part One: West of War

by
John Hartigan Waldo

2017

Table of Contents

Author's Note...

Both of my grandmothers were named Mary, but only one fought spies and pirates during World War One.

Some long-neglected letters, postcards, photographs, and souvenirs came to light recently, so that family legends of missing years, mysterious friends, and unaccounted journeys could be pieced together.

Historical persons and events mentioned in this narrative, especially where it departs from common knowledge, are treated in end notes; other people depicted in this story have succeeded in hiding from history.

I can show you the pictures, but I'd rather tell you this story...

CHAPTER 1
A Missing Man

POST CARD

FOR CORRESPONDENCE • 2 FOR ADDRESS ONLY

NEW YORK APR 27 1915

C

U.S. POSTAGE

Arrived Grand Central
Station this morning.
Ruth met me.
Will telegraph news.

Nova Haines
705 East Eighth Street
Kansas City, Missouri

"No word of him in three weeks?"

Sisterly hugs and pecks on the cheeks were exchanged, then Mary fell into step beside Ruth, motioned to the redcap, and with high-buttoned boots clicking across the polished stone floor, they strode towards the distant Forty-second Street doors, through the columns of sunlight streaming from Grand Central's high windows, making a classical golden atmosphere of the cigar and cigarette smoke.

I'd forgotten what a glorious transition this Station makes for a traveler entering New York City, thought Mary.[1]

"Nova's frantic. She's telegraphed twice since Friday. I wish she could come East with us," said Ruth.[2]

"She can't leave the business. I've brought more photographs, including their wedding portrait. Postcard from Mister Haines, postmarked New York City, is the last word from him."

"Don't get them out here. There's a fellow in a bowler hat on the mezzanine studying us through field glasses, the Italian following us on our right quarter is an informant for the Black Hand, and the one-eyed man who was crowding in to eavesdrop is Hafiz the Persian. I almost got him when I swung my umbrella carelessly," said Ruth .

"Ruth! What have you been about in New York, to attract such ruffians?"

"Did like you told me with the money you sent," said Ruth.

"I've been telephoning and writing the New York and Cuba Mail Line, and the other shippers on the southern trade routes. Then I hired a detective for inquiries in Havana, where the big prize-fight was held."

"What was so important about one prize fight," asked Mary, "that seventy thousand spectators sat in the bright sun at the Oriental Race Track to watch 'The Great White Hope' beat Jack Johnson?"

"He drove his automobile with his wife to Chicago," objected Ruth. "She's white; he's a tall, confident black man, who makes millions thrashing other men, most of them white. If he ever sets foot in this country, the Federal authorities will imprison him for that so-called violation of the Mann Act."

"The Kaiser would get a better reception in this country," suggested Mary. "Even if he marched with the Wobblies."

"Ix-Nay," hissed Ruth. "The man in the Homburg who just passed us is plain-clothes NYPD. Anyway, my detective called the jails and hospitals and hotels in Havana - no William Haines. He had to, I have no Spanish."

"Hmm, we share this Hemisphere with a hundred million speakers of Español, as many as speak English in the New World," said Mary. "It would be worth the study, I think."

She continued while they walked.

"My Kansas students were talking about the European War on my last day teaching: I told them that we must study History (that's History, with a capital 'H') or, as the Spanish philosopher Senõr Santayana recently wrote, (translated to English) we'll be forced to repeat it. A little boy's eyes lit up, and he proclaimed, 'This time I'm going to be a pirate!'

"I'm not going back to teaching."

"Well, maybe this will be the summer we catch a millionaire or an actor," said Ruth.

"Or a cop or a grocer," finished Mary. "Remember Zeisloft's seven levels of wealth in New York City. I know we aren't among the submerged poor, so are we...?" She thought how Aunt Clem had married Charles Morse, whose Wall Street speculations had long since placed him among the very rich.

"Let's get you settled, get to the office, and we can start planning what to do," said Ruth. "Stick close to me until you re-gain your sense of City traffic. Almost three times as many fatalities in New York City street accidents this year as were murdered here. Just makes me wonder how many traffic deaths are deliberate murder."

3

All Mary's baggage, including a bulky trunk, nearly desk-sized, re-inforced with wood strakes and pressed-steel corners, required a taxi-cab, were piled in. The two young women leaned back as the cab turned south.

Mary enjoyed the luxury of a cab ride through miles of heavy morning traffic of delivery trucks, steam-wagons, horse drays and carriages, and occasional horse-back riders, even some push-carts, along with electric sedans, sputtering gasoline runabouts, all dodging trolley cars passing swiftly back and forth, and the other vehicles, all shuffling downtown, directed by traffic cops at the main intersections.

And this is a Sunday morning, thought Mary.

"You noticed those two fellows in brown three-piece suits, with the high bowler hats, who moved in on our redcap as we got in the cab?"

"Yes, Mary, thanks for not discussing that while we were riding.

They'll likely interview our cabbie; they're part of the same crowd watching me ever since I hired the detective," said Ruth. "I think they were some of Burns' detectives, judging how they dressed..."

"Hmm. Reading too many issues of the 'National Police Gazette'?"

"Growing up in our part of Missoura, I wouldn't hire Pinkertons, do you think? They're still asking people where 'Mister Howard' buried his gold, and Jesse in his grave since the year you were born."

Mary interrupted. "That's not the year I was born, and don't you forget it, younger sister."

"Fine. Although, anymore, they're edging away from labor warfare, back to the Treasury Department, just as Burns prefers to hire out with the Justice Department and the U.S. Attorney-General. I thought the shadowers just represented the rival agencies checking each other's business, after my agent reported both groups asked him questions about me."

"I 'd like to hire Mollie Babbitt, or 'Tish' Carberry, or better yet, call up 'The Girl At Central' and ask her what's going on, and the World's Greatest Detective has retired."

"Nonsense, Mary, he's exactly your age," jibed Ruth. She frowned slightly.

"Ma Markowitz told me some odd people have 'phoned asking for me every day. She said they reminded her of the Tsar's secret police back in the old country. They won't leave a message so she just blesses them in Yiddish and hangs up.

"You know, the Tsar's secret police, the Okhrana: they hire American detectives to watch and maybe harass the Russian immigrants. They fear the immigrants conspire to topple the Tsar."

Mary laughed.

"You should write for the 'Police Gazette, Ruth."

"We're lucky to get this room in her boarding house again this summer. Let's get over to the office." She threw on a light green linen coat, stuck a small straw hat covered with artificial flowers in her coiled light- brown hair with long sharp hatpins of 20-gauge tempered steel wire.

At the new Automat, they dropped nickels to open little glass doors allowing access to bowls of tomato soup, chicken sandwiches, and fresh apple pie. A nickel-plated classical dolphin spouted coffee into cups.

"Hot and getting hotter. Paper says record heat this weekend," said Ruth.

"Whatever you do, don't mention ice when we call on Charlie Morse."[3]

"No, I won't; it's good of him to give his wife's shirt-tail relations such a good job and I trust you noticed the Burns Bowler Boys across the street, staring," murmured Ruth.

"And the slight, well-dressed man in the Panama hat walking behind us may be Cuban or Brazilian, but he's reading a Yiddish newspaper upside-down," observed Mary. "Ooh, he almost walked into that beer truck that came around the corner."

"You spotted that Japanese diplomat-type earlier in Grand Central. Did you recognize that New York City Police detective who just passed by? Still think I'm reading too much in the 'Police Gazette'?"

"We'll catch a trolley at the corner; see who tries to follow," decided Mary.

* * *

A tarantula waved at Rafael X. Neel, from where it rode on the hundred-and-seventy-seventh bunch of bananas the lean black man had carried ashore on his shoulder this morning.

6

"Welcome to New York City," wheezed 'Raff', as he carefully lowered his burden onto the waiting rail car. "I'll play one-seventy-seven today," he promised the creature, already scrambling for concealment in the dark, as the man swung back down the gangway.

"Didn't I win last week on ninety-seven, on your cousin's advice?" His friend Archie claimed he'd seen black children begging wholesalers to let them rescue tropical spiders from stacks of bananas fresh off the boats; take them home to keep down the cockroaches and rats in their tenements.

The whole scheme had collapsed when one enterprising young man was seen to bring in his own collection of tarantulas, which he would guarantee to remove at five for a penny. Only in this town.

And there is the lad himself, as the Irishmen liked to say.

"Josephus," called the 'longshoreman. "One-seven-seven!" And the skinny kid with the winning grin, whose swift hand had snatched the quarter-dollar out of the air replied, "One seven seven, Mister Neel."

Yes sir, we're all hustlers.

Soon enough, unloading was done, and the 'banana fiends' started to drift toward the paymaster's window. Time to follow up some other business.

The "One Big Union" needed organizers and recruiters, but he wouldn't have to go all the way up to their office on Eighty-first Street. Closer in, the Cunard dicks paid eyes and ears to follow Germans, Socialists, Irishmen, Anarchists, and Hindoos. Martin, of the TransAtlantique Line wanted a lead on sabotage, he's probably an agent with French Sûrete or the Deuxième Bureau.

Don't forget the Gophers, and the River Rats; they'd grant passage through their territory for good tips of poorly-guarded trucks and doors.

And the Germans!

The Germans were positively throwing money around the docks just for warnings, minor errands, and cartage of small parcels.

Frank Tunney's man from the New York Bomb Squad was expecting some names.

Something about May Day next Saturday tickled the back of his head. Or was it just another spider looking for safety, heh heh. Raff whipped his coat over his shoulder anyway and headed Uptown.

* * *

"There's our boat! The 'C.W. Morse'.[4] Floating at the pier like a big white swan."

"And all summer, she'll race up the River, skimming the waves like a whole flock of swans."

"We should commission an ad with a painting of swans flying alongside with the 'C.W. Morse!'"

The People's Line building, three stories of brick stained by river, tides, and storms, controlled access to the River excursion steamers operating at Pier 32 on the Hudson River.

"No-one here but the watchmen; Sunday," explained Ruth. "I know our folks worry about us not keeping the Sabbath; maybe I should tell them we've joined Pastor Porter's Big Church in the Middle of the Block?"

"Old joke, they've heard it. We can attend services aboard the boat this summer."

Mary and Ruth chatted for a few minutes with the guard at the Eleventh Street entrance, mentioning their concern for their missing brother-in-law, and displaying a recent photo pasted on a cardboard backing, showing William Haines.

The guard sympathized, and said, "Miss Cowles, the Cuba mail boat gets in today. Recent passenger lists will be available."

Mary thanked him while Ruth unlocked the door to the second-floor staircase, where the purser's office was located. Walking upstairs, she switched on the incandescent lights, carried a stack of newspapers and letters over to the roll-top desk and work table by the North windows.

"And we're back on the Hudson River for the summer, Mary," said Ruth, unlatching and pushing open windows.

"The boating season starts next week, early, because of the Navy Review by President Wilson. We must look over the new crewlists of the excursion boats, sign in with the Bank for cash transport, check with the steward on the food vendors' charge accounts, and meet with the Musician's Union representatives for the onboard dance bands."

"How about the printers?"

"Tickets, claimchecks, postcards and brochures, handbills for the 1915 season, should be here tomorrow for approval, then bulk deliveries for payment by certified check by Thursday afternoon," said Ruth. "Brochures and postcards approved, arriving tomorrow."

Ruth motioned to the recent newspapers, sheets opened and hanging over both sides of the big work table under a framed four-foot by two-foot bright-colored lithograph of a modern sidewheel steamer racing the wind up the Hudson.

"I'm checking our advertisements in all the City's newspapers," said Ruth. "And I'm clipping out the steamer schedules to Cuba.

"I paid 50 dollars cash to Lew Daniels, down by Pier Seventeen. He hires out plain-clothes guards for the excursion boats, the banana boats, and the Hidalgo Trading people, and he has contacts among the waterfront gangs and the river pirates. Here's his second report, just arrived," she said, picking up a manila envelope from the desk.

"I've renewed our firearms permits for New York City at the Police Commissioner's office. Here's yours. And I bought a brace of new Austrian Schwartzlose automatics in .32 caliber from Warner's. See, you push the slide forward to charge it. Supposed to be less recoil when you fire."

Mary considered.

"We'll be handling so much money on the boats this summer, I'll rely on my short-barreled railroad revolver. I can't work dum-dums through an automatic."

"Why would you need dum-dums, teaching school in Kansas?"

"I'm starting to look on it as thirteen wasted years. I've taught school there since I was sixteen, even when I was attending Normal college for teachers off-season.

"And farm work doesn't interest me much anymore; planting oats behind our mules last week at the folks' farm."

"Well, thanks for helping Papa on your way out here," Ruth interjected.

"May oats are up in Chicago," Mary continued. "Or I should say, oat futures are up, not the crop. Papa expects that the War will raise grain prices, and he'd rather feed the mules and horses of Missouri, than sell them to France and Russia, like our neighbors are doing. Buyers all over the Midwest who supply the British mission. Imagine Maud and Jack pulling cannons in the trenches."

"Going to be a boom market," suggested Ruth.

"Maybe travel," Mary mused. "I want to see more than Kansas.

"I teach geography out of Mister Dodge's book, and I'd like to see the Mountains of the Moon, visit the Alps, and the Grand Canal, and the Southern Ocean, maybe see the elephant when she's at home on the Irrawaddy River..."

Ruth skimmed through the report from the detective agency, and hurriedly picked up the 'phone set.

"Hello, Central, get me Barratry...oh, pardon me, I mean, Battery Twenty-one-seven-nine, please... they're ringing... Yes, hello, Mister Daniels, this is Ruth Cowles at Peoples' Line... we received your report and..." Ruth listened for a moment, pressed her lips into a thin, hard line, then hung up without another word.

"He's abandoned our case; he won't even discuss it. Orders, he said."

"So this is the champion who faced down the Tongs and broke into the River Rats and the Green Hand?" scoffed Mary. "We might have made a mistake, hiring that detective. He's talking to other parties about us," she said. "We'll have to continue on our own, and we must conclude investigations this week. Our excursion boats start running next week; there'll be no more time."

A few minutes later, Mary had typed up an outline for a poster: Reward, for information on where-abouts of William Haines of Kansas City, who passed through New York City bound for the prize fight in Havana in early April, with a description, a City post office box, and her name. Mary held up the sheet.

"I think we should pay extra and get his picture printed on this, maybe send copies to all the detective agencies in town," she said.

"Most of the big detective agencies work for both sides of the European War, as the belligerents conspire in our neutral country."

Ruth saw Mary's startled look, and went on. "They sell names and secrets to the Central Powers and the Allies both, as well as engage in small-scale violence and crime on their behalf right here in New York City. Sometimes, not so small-scale."

"If we're on the spot, and run out of ideas and leads maybe we can work that to our advantage. Let the people with information become anxious to talk to us," said Mary.

"We'll need more staff for the excursion boats this summer. When we call on Local One-Twenty-Three tomorrow, let's ask about their band members who play on the mail boats to Cuba. That could give us an approach to interview crew members who might have seen Mister Haines," finished Mary.

"Good!" Ruth went on, "We can visit the East River docks tomorrow, beginning with the Seaman's Refuge Church. Sister O'Shea will help us with introductions, and post flyers for us with her contacts. Also, call at the Longshoreman's Rest on this side of town."

"I've promised to meet some young men from the Radio Club this afternoon over at New York University in the Bronx. We might ask them to pass the word on their wireless network; they have so many contacts."

"We'll go together," agreed Mary. "Let's type copies of our Reward Notice, carbons, too, for the print shops. We'll distribute them all day tomorrow, while we make calls for the Company."

* * *

From the worn seat of his little junk wagon Abie Greenberg guided his tired old horse through the crowded streets of the Lower East Side, between push carts, street games, spilled garbage, stalled delivery trucks; pushing past an almost solid barrier of noise: horns, alarm bells, sirens, klaxons, backfiring automobiles, the grind of streetcar wheels, boat whistles from the East River, families shouting at their children, their landlords, or their tenants, cops shouting at pushcart vendors, and a dog or two barking.

And the smell! Thirteen years in America after leaving the Old Country, and he still couldn't accept the sewers, the Rivers, dead animals in the street, vendor food raw or cooked, dinners being prepared over oil fires, kerosene, or gas or electric ranges; wood smoke, coal smoke, ozone from electric wires, half-million human bodies in a quarter-mile radius; but just now, a breeze from the Sea. That's so much better.

He pulled up on the reins to give a young black man a chance to scramble up on the seat with him.

"Thank you, Mister Greenberg. How goes it with you?"

"Good afternoon, Mister Neel," answered Abie. He knew his passenger better as Raff, or 'Rags', for his rag factory work, but junk dealers, collectors of rags, bottles, and scrap found a little formality and polite speech helped smooth their haggling.

"Just this morning, a coil of thin steel wire, only slightly rusty, a penny, I might get 2 cents for, but my boy, Isaac, calls himself 'Tom Swift' on the air, wants a bigger aerial for his 'wireless' machine, I don't understand it, but he's a good boy, wants to study electrical engineering in college; maybe we'll get him a place with Edison Electric, eh?"

Raff gave an agreeable smile, and reached into his coat pocket.

"Here's a couple of complimentary passes to the Hippodrome Show. Two bananas, just off the boat, Mister Greenberg; and this note for Mister Gleaves at the Union Hall when you stop there; he'll have something else for you, too. I'll drop off at the corner. Thanks."

And he was gone, lost in the crowd. Raff had another pass to tonight's 'Hippodrome' show and figured he could use some entertainment with his people in the upper gallery there.

* * *

Pausing to drop a picture postcard into the corner mailbox, Ruth had time for a glimpse of the sidewalk behind, with no definite result, so she pulled out another stamped postcard, scrawled a brief message of greetings and love to her parents in Missouri.

"This street-car line will get us across to the East Side. It's time to get aboard, and observe if anyone hurries to catch up," she said.

Mary just glanced at her sister in amusement.

"No, really, then we'll transfer and drop in on that print shop I 'phoned. They're Jewish, so they keep a different Sabbath than ours."

Shortly, somewhat East of Broadway, Ruth handed in their copy.

"The Tsar's agents buy ad space in some of our local newspapers exhorting our readers to purchase Russian war bonds, but I doubt if my fellow immigrants will forget the pogram at Kishinev, nu?" said Fedor Povitch, as he picked up a type stick, and began to arrange tiny lead characters, while monitoring the big rotary press, and rushing to answer a jangling telephone, then shouting into it over the noise, in what seemed to Mary as several languages at once.

"I'll set type while we finish the run on this new Socialist weekly in Yiddish, 'Forverts', Abe Cahan will call for it today. He operates on a shoestring, so we give him a good price on newsprint, too."

Swiftly filling the type stick, he smiled at Mary and Ruth, and pointed.

"There's my cousin upstairs; he'll do me the photo etching. Two hundred copies, or would you like five hundred copies for another buck? No? Okay, ready by five o'clock; thanks," he finished as Mary handed him a two-and-a half dollar gold Indian.

Mary and Ruth stepped out into a noon-time battered by a cruel unseasonal sun.

"Now we stop at A & P, or the first deli we see, for picnic supplies, before crossing the East River," decided Ruth.

"Everybody else is closed for Sunday, so tomorrow we'll drop copies at all the foreign consulates, buy ads in the newspapers in English; we can't afford translations. We should know by the end of the week if any answer will turn up."

"I've been thinking, Mary. What if Billy Haines fell in with political intriguers, maybe serving as a courier for them while covering it with the trip to the prize fight? He had opinions, and talked pretty loud."

"How could it hurt to get involved with politics? He's probably just run off and left Nova, but I'm not bringing it up with her until we've made reasonable attempts to find him, okay?"

Post Card

Hall of Fame of Notable Americans
at New York University, the Bronx

Place
Stamp
Here

Mama, Papa, we're going to be in the Hall of Fame!
– Ruth

Calvin and Augusta Cowles.

Auxvasse, Missouri

Ruth and Mary got out of their taxicab in front of the library building at New York University, on the Heights. Mary wondered if this had figured in General Washington's defense of New York.

Overlooking a commanding view of the East River and Manhattan and carrying a large cloth bag filled with deli food, Ruth and Mary marched along under the welcome shade of the columned open portico: The Hall of Fame of Notable Americans, heroes and heroines of the Arts: Literary, Mechanical, Political, and more, to a group of students, a few girls among them, gathered in front of the bronze bust of Samuel F.B. Morse.

Introductions were made by a tall, lanky gentleman slightly older than the rest. But the crazy, uncombed hair made him look younger.

"These worthies are 'Frank Read' and 'Frank Merriwell', these 'the Rover Boys', here the 'Wireless Boys', after the juvenile fiction series, here's Li Lian, 'the Lily of the Lightnings', 'Tom Swift', and Tom's sisters Dejah and Thuvia, as they sign themselves on the air, (a couple of real farbrente Yidische meydlekh)," Mary thought she heard him finish under his breath.

"And I'm Hugo Gernsbach, at your service, ma'am," said the elder of the group.[5]

"'Electrical Experimenter' magazine?" asked Mary. "My students tear through every issue that arrives in Kansas."

Gernsbach grinned at the compliment.

"We hope to be part of building a worldwide network of free unencumbered communications on the air, like having free telegraph or telephone service. If radio sets can stay inexpensive…"

"And not overly regulated," interrupted Harry, youngest of the self-styled 'Rover Boys'. "Our State Department already restricts coded messages leaving the United States, to protect U.S. Neutrality, and we're pretty sure the U.S. Navy monitors wireless traffic."

One of the 'Wireless Boys' spoke up, "To give you some more background, ladies, the British and Italian governments demand that the U.S. Government shut down the world's most powerful transmitter, out at Sayville, run by Telefunken, the big German company formed by the Kaiser's Imperial Command just before the War."

"Why? At the risk of sounding uninformed," asked Ruth.

"Wireless is already Big Business," pontificated brother Tom, "as well as a National Security issue: remember the ongoing lawsuit between Marconi and Tesla, and the wide public promotion of Signor Marconi as the sole inventor of radio? Well, the U.S. Navy prefers not to rely on foreign patents, so they have adopted Professor Tesla's American patents."

"Yes, he demonstrated radio equipment, and filed years before Marconi," added Harry. "The Navy also wants any developments of Dr. Tesla's remote- control vehicles, or the Death-Ray."

"Death-ray, fiddlesticks," said Tom Swift heatedly. "Professor Pupin says..."

"Ah, yes, enter the other Serbian savant," said Frank Read, raising his hand for peace, and smiling to re-assure the outsiders. "Professor Mikhail Pupin is Columbia University's Chair of Mechanics, including electricity. Also Honorary Consul of the Kingdom of Serbia."

At that moment a nearby church bell rang, and instantly the Radio Club members bowed in different directions. Gernsbach nodded toward the 'Wireless Boys'.

"Genuflecting toward His laboratory in the Woolworth Building, while Frank Merriwell gives obeisance to Menlo Park, Langley Collyer here hopes to study with Professor Pupin ..."

Everyone watched Frank Read and the three 'Rover Boys', Tom, Dick, and Harry, who waved their hands in the air, chanting "Steinmetz! Steinmetz! Gimme a square root of negative One! Yeah!", and threw themselves on the pavement to kow-tow towards distant Schenectady, while the whole group dissolved in laughter.

Mary and Ruth passed around bottles of Dr. Brown's, and a big carton of bagels and cream cheese.

Thuvia accepted a bagel and turned to the Cowles sisters.

"That's the kind of nonsense that started this whole terrible European War. Professor Pupin's uneasy with Nicola Tesla's natural genius and visionary inspiration; he teaches that only a mathematical approach will lead to advances in electricity.

"And Pupin distrusts Tesla for being friendly with everyone, including the Germans, which is why J.P. Morgan stopped funding Tesla."

Mary and Ruth just listened, and tried not to feel overwhelmed by the energy of the radio enthusiasts.

"Then there's Tesla's giant transmitter. He could turn that machine to any use," added Dick.

"Dick knows I'm saving money to attend Columbia University," said Frank Read. "That's why he's smirking."

"Yeah, Frank," said Thuvia, "remember Columbia's motto: 'In lumine tuo videbemus lumen', you know: 'In Your light, we shall see the light.' Ick."

"Death Rays, again, Thuvia? You're just being pessimistic."

"No, if you build it, someone will use it on the poor soldiers, or more likely, the proletariat," insisted Thuvia. "One of Steinmetz' students, maybe Edwin Scott? He claims to have a working model."

"A Death Ray?" asked Mary, in some doubt.

"An electric cannon," explained Hugo Gernsbach. "Like H.G. Wells' Martian Heat Ray, or perhaps shooting streams of highly-charged metal particles at distant battleships or Zeppelins."

"The Martians don't need to invade Earth," said Thuvia. "The whole continent of Europe is the playground of Mars, the God of War."

"You should write that for 'The Masses' paper over there," said Frank Read, nodding toward Manhattan.

Gernsbach waved his hands to call the meeting back to order.

"I'm sure you ladies have thought about the political implications of your inquiries? After we start spreading the word, you'll be amazed at how wide a net we cast tonight - we borrow fishermen's terms for 'network' and 'broadcasting'.

"We can publicize your search and your reward for information, strictly as an unpaid experiment. You should know that seven thousand listeners may tune in, and you may get more attention than you expect."

Mary and Ruth exchanged looks, hoping not to give too much away.

Gernsbach spoke up, "All in favor of assisting the Cowles sisters with their search, raise your hands? Unanimous. One A.M. Greenwich. Good luck, ladies."

Hugo Gernsbach wondered if he could interview Professor Tesla or this Edwin Scott fellow, maybe publish plans and sell parts for the Death Ray; no, every boy in America would build one, look at how radio is catching on.

In his head, Gernsbach calculated small equipment costs for the 'electrical séance' set, like the one he'd built for Harry Houdini. Head phones wired to antennae to pick up disembodied spirit voices from Outside; thought is electrical in nature, right? Then some pocket torches with tinted lenses to make a medium's eyes glow red, as though possessed by evil spirits.

Ugh.

Hadn't there been unsettling rumors about Houdini's 'electrical séance', with some young man hearing bad sounds and stumbling away, to the horror of every dog and horse he passed?

He thought about lighting effects. Maybe an electric halo. William Jennings Bryan might like one. Or that beautiful Suffragette who rides a white horse in the parades. A simple mist sprayer made of stamped tin to create a faint cloud, and a diffused light beam to play behind the holy one's head. Just a subtle glow, not a big searchlight. What about those Hindoo swamis lecturing in town, or the fakirs or dervishes? Or maybe try out this new patent, the neon light?

Charge enough to selected clients, rather than advertise and make everyone aware of the trick. Stage productions, opera, vaudeville. Would Harry Houdini mind?

"Pleased to meet you, too, Miss Cowles," said Hugo Gernsbach. "And you, too, Ruth, as my friend Davidson would remind me of correct forms."

After some exchanges of technical advice and new call signs and wave-lengths, the radio club members dispersed, to prepare for classes and work on Monday. One member found a telephone, another passed word to his contact in the Serbian Black Hand, and somebody else called up Hafiz, who went down his client list, made two reports to detective agencies, mailed a written report to a Federal department, 'phoned three members of foreign consulates, including a member of the Serbian White Hand, and then went to a meeting in a German beer hall.

* * *

"I'm told that 'Seventy-Eight' and 'Eighty-Six' are radio shorthand endearments, Mary," advised Ruth. "That nice 'Tom Rover' with the wavy hair, asked for my 'phone number. Gave him our business office number, since they're being so helpful. Notice how Frank Read gave Thuvia a ride on his motorcycle? She uses '2VA' as her call sign."

Ruth scanned the campus.

"We can catch a jitney at the bottom of the hill to get us back to Midtown."

"Sounds like a disease to catch, or some vile habit," said Mary.

"No, I read it's slang for a nickel, the regular fare. Everybody wants an automobile, so people figure ways to support such an expensive machine."

"Maybe they'll start delivering food, just like the trucks of the Postal Service are trying out," Mary said.

After a while, Mary spoke up again. " Let's pick up the printing on our way home, and call at Suffragette Headquarters. A meeting's scheduled for all afternoon, so I know they're open," said Ruth. "Aunt Clem introduced me to Carrie Catt, who's taken leadership again of National American Women Suffrage Association." Mary nodded for Ruth to continue.

"New plans to raise funds, increase membership, and get 'Votes For Women' on the ballot this Fall. We can canvas for the Cause all week while we make our other calls."

"Why?"

"Come, now, Mary," said Ruth a little sharply. "You'd suggest women don't have a stake in this Nation?"

"Just making sure of our commitment. And that's an argument we'll use with immigrants from down South, where it's dangerous to vote, and with folks from overseas, where they've never had any rights at all.

"This is the year," finished Mary.

Their ride, a Ford truck, roughly fitted with old trolley benches, or church pews, looked like, thought Mary, bore a chalked sign on the rattling engine cover: 'Knox Avenue Bridge – Manhattanville'.

"Thanks, ladies," said the driver, the original 'Gasoline Gus', accepting their nickels, and revving up to pull into traffic.

"The monopoly men, y'know, the trolley companies, the busses, and IRT, and taxi companies hate us jitneys, and demand that the City and Albany push all three thousand of us out of town," he assured Mary, Ruth, and the other six passengers, looking back at them often as he dodged horse carts, trucks, streetcars, and pedestrians desperately trying to run across the street.

The lack of any encouragement beyond worried smiles just seemed to make Gus more talkative and less concerned about the traffic.

"So we're looking for work as couriers around Town, or maybe we'll deliver pizzas, or Chinese food or deli food, waddaya think?"

"Eighth Avenue, Mary. We can catch the Elevated all the way down to Headquarters."

"We'll drop in on the Musician's Union; we need to talk to them about signing bands for the boats; oh, there's another of the big printed banners on that 'bus, advertising bonds for sale to support, uh, 'The Second Austro-Hungarian War Loan', at six per cent interest."

Ruth made a wry face.

"I could get better returns throwing money down the sewer grating I think. But why look? The whole town is covered with handbills, posters for theaters, movies, patent-medicines. "All these buildings show signs painted in black and white directly on the bricks, hotel names, ads for furniture, hand cream; there's one for 'Gopher Brand Tonic', whatever that is. You'll get your City sense back soon and you won't see those, nor be bothered by the constant hum, or roar, of city life."

"Here's a stop: the 'Longshoreman's Rest'. We can't enter, but Joe, the doorman, he'll take a couple of our handbills," Mary said. "Good afternoon, Mister O'Hara. Mary and Ruth Cowles."

"We're with 'Peoples' Line' again this season. A handbill I hope you'll post on the bulletin board, and this envelope for the collection, please."

Joe smiled and nodded.

A couple minutes commenting on the unexpected heat wave, and they continued walking.

"Sun's getting low, let's head home. I don't want to be chloroformed by the white slavers, or Doctor Mors, or Fantômas and the Vampire Gang," said Ruth.

Mary laughed nervously.

"Doctor Mors has vanished, the Vampire Robbers are just a movie serial, and I doubt if the French Sûrete or Deuxième Bureau really set Fantômas working against Teutonic spies in North America."

"Well, they should," suggested Ruth. "We'll take the pastrami sandwiches home, please," she said in the next deli, handing over a greenback for change.

"Saboteurs are burning ships carrying munitions and supplies to the French and British armies. I read how police in New Orleans caught a bomber sneaking a clockwork bomb into a cargo ship earlier this year. It's not just thriller fiction."

"Good, we're home," Mary announced, and pushed the door shut on the sun setting in red and orange glory behind the Manhattan skyline.

CHAPTER TWO
Jungle Sorceress

Lucia and her partner Aludra were each twenty-seven years of age, and had worked many other acts in show business, Aludra usually in more clothing than her 'Jungle Princess' effect created by a casually-draped leopard skin, a bonnet of tall feathers, and a thin cloak of brilliant silk, and Lucia usually in quite a bit less than the colorful and enormous robe thrown over her shoulders. Both saluted the audience, Aludra with a graceful wave of a slim brown arm, Lucia curling her trunk and raising a forefoot.

Lucia reached over to the easel standing at stage left and plucked out a white poster-board bearing the title:

> # "ANIMALS PERFORMING MAGIC"

holding it up to announce the act, as rows of electric bulbs in wide panels left and right of the Hippodrome's stage repeated the title, and Aludra went into her spiel.

"Animals perform illusion and magic to survive in their daily lives," Aludra explained in a clear, slow tone, stretching out her hands to persuade, as an assistant brought out a large open basket of wicker, which Aludra tilted to show it contained three white rabbits.

"You've seen flocks of birds flashing about to make hawks miss their mark, schools of fish swirling around to fake out sharks and barracudas; herds of antelopes or zebra dodging back and forth to confuse lions."

"Our earliest magicians studied the movements of birds and animals and how they use distraction and deception to escape predators."

"Please watch their best tricks up close," and she picked up a rabbit, who made no objection as she swirled a scarf of brilliant silk in circles over it, then swept the scarf aside to reveal no rabbit.

Aludra took another bunny in her hands, covered it for a moment with the swirling scarf, instantly swept away to reveal: no bunny.

Applause started to grow.

"It looks like the Forces of Magic favor us tonight," announced the sorceress. "Shall we make sure?"

This time Aludra handed her long cloak of red, green, and gold silk to Lucia, who draped the cloak over a third rabbit held by Aludra, then swirled it away to show Aludra's suddenly empty hands.

Applause filled the cavernous Hippodrome as Aludra held up the wicker basket to reveal all three rabbits comfortably contained.

Lucia picked up the basket by its sturdy central handle and passed it to an assistant heading back to the wings. The elephant picked out another card from the easel, and held it up for the audience to read:

"SWEPT AWAY BY BIRDS"

as stage hands rolled out tall wire cages filled with bright-feathered little birds chirping and twitting and hopping from perch to perch.

Aludra put her hand on Lucia's shoulder for a moment, then glided away into the center of the semi-circle of bird cages.

Fluorishing her silken cloak, Aludra raised it before her in a sudden motion, and Lucia stamped her left front foot, and trumpeted, filling the hall with echoes as the cages snapped open to fill the air around Aludra with a whirling cloud of colorful finches and parakeets who flew up out of sight into the space above the stage.

The silken cloak drifted to the floor and settled flat.

Now mystified silence reigned in the Hippodrome, stretching out for a four-count, until a spotlight caught Aludra perched on a trapeze, descending from the fly loft above her starting place.

Unrestrained cheers and explosions of hand-clapping as Lucia returned the applause with bowing and waving.

Lucia reached and held up another card:

> "WATCH ME
> VANISH
> THE GIRL"

which produced spontaneous cheers as the audience grasped the promise.

Lucia reached back, pulled a cord to release the big embroidered curtain to drop down from her back, concealing her sides and legs, right down to her red-painted toenails, and she shifted to present her left side to the crowd, and curled her trunk against her cheek thoughtfully.

Aludra stepped in front, smiling and talking confidently to Lucia and the audience, made a curtsey and slipped behind Lucia's big red wrap.

Lucia reached, and held up another card:

> "WATCH
> CLOSELY
> PLEASE"

She trumpeted twice, and let the big cloth drop to the floor.

No sign of Aludra.

The audience started to applaud, and Lucia waved her trunk and shuffled around to show that no girl was hiding behind her, nor under her. She stamped twice on the coverlet to suggest that nobody could hide there.

A moment of silence, then truly thunderous applause and cheers, and whistles, acknowledged by Lucia's trumpets, hoots, and squeals.

Aludra suddenly ran out from stage left, hugged Lucia around one great leg, to sustained applause.

More bows, and Aludra made sure to step back, gesturing toward the elephant, and let Lucia take applause all for herself; then final curtain, and Lucia and Aludra walked off the stage, listening to the producer's enthusiastic reaction.

"Miss Ada, it's a *solid* magic act; clever twist having the animals perform the magic themselves, good pacing, moved right along. Birds all back in their cages, very smooth. And your 'Jungle Sorceress' image is exotic, maybe South Seas, South Africa, or South America, perfectly mysterious, even though you live in South Jersey."

Ada nodded.

"Thank you, Mister Dillingham."

"And you know how the owners, from young Fred Thompson to these current people; they all want new acts to employ our menagerie of big animals we keep here in the Hippodrome. Otherwise, they'll be...dispersed, maybe to foreign acts."

Ada set her lips firmly to avoid reacting to that thought.

"Maybe Mister Thompson will take us at the San Francisco Expo. I hear he means to take back operation of his Toyland concession. He's always liked elephants. I can take time off from my day job typing at N-double-A-CP, downtown."

The producer shook his head, and said, "Instead, how about twelve weeks here, nightly, plus Saturday matinee, look over this renewable contract; let me know to-morrow, hm?"

"Oh! Thank you, Mister Dillingham. Now they're going to take Lucia downstairs."

The producer caught the unspoken feeling, said nothing else, smiled re-assurance, and watched Ada talk to Lucia until the wranglers came up.

* * *

Hours later, Raff found rest in his waterfront garret, after deciding "gonna marry me that Jungle Princess."

CHAPTER THREE
"What This Country Really Needs..."
or
"Sometimes A Zeppelin Is Only A Zeppelin."

"Smokes," said Hafiz, the One-eyed Persian. "Burns," replied a stout blond man, puffing on a cheroot as he emerged from the 5-AM shadows of the alley behind Hartigan's Bar, while the Elevated rumbled overhead at Chatham Square.
Hafiz handed over a new cigar box bearing the bright lithographed labels proclaiming:

> ## "NEW YORK'S MARY ROGERS"
> ## and
> ## "MARY ROGERS BRAND"

and depicting the beautiful cigar girl Mary brandishing a handful of cigars amidst Nineteenth-Century buildings.

His delivery made, Hafiz accepted a small envelope and crossed the street for his next delivery and another job. His favorite work place, Hammerstein's 'Victoria', was closing, and the new owners had announced they would re-open in a week as a full-time movie palace.

Hafiz threw shining knives that flashed in the air, from both hands at once, one to strike a match fastened to a target to ignite a big stogie cigar just about it, just trimmed by the other knife, then, placing the cigar to his lips to puff twice while bowing to the crowd.

Hafiz had worked many acts in vaudeville, under many names, including his own, Kevin O'Connor. Time to get out of the circuit of vaudeville, so he'd given his assistant two months' notice, and she'd already opened a new magic act at the Hippodrome last night. Pretty good, he thought, and he must telegraph congratulations.

* * *

Manhattan, in the Bowl of Night, wasn't even roaring yet, as Morning cast the stone to put the Stars to flight, thought Mary, already dressed in a coat of light brown linen. Checked her heavy cloth purse while Ruth unlocked the door of their third-floor flat. Very little light from a feeble bulb up the dim hall, but enough to show the stairway.

Both young women returned Mrs. Markowitz's smile at the front door when she cautioned them:

"Watch out crossing the streets, you're new in the city, those wild young men from Uptown, they race their runabouts like they drive the Rockefeller; and the truckers! Doesn't matter if they drive horses or steam or gazoline or electric: thundering down te Avenues, whipping around corners like the Cossacks upon our villages.

"Sure you can't take breakfast here? So early, and the ferries to Jersey every ten minutes. Some cocoa, a couple eggs. Good, sit, now, and I explain how suffragettes need black women involved. Then I give you addresses to their churches, OK?" said Mrs. Markowitz without pausing for breath.

Fortified by a meal, Mary and Ruth sat on the upper deck in the brisk air of early morning and felt the tide and sea breeze kick up a little chop against the North River's steady current.

" 'And Lo! The Hunter of the East has caught, the Sultan's turret in a Noose of Light!'," Mary quoted, pointing past the bow of the Fort Lee ferry at the tall cliffs of the Palisades, glowing in the rays of the sunrise over Manhattan.

Ruth shrugged.

"Omar and Fitzgerald's Rubaiyat, of course," explained Mary.

"Oh, that's Mister Laemmle's new studio. Light flashing off the glass walls, through the trees. Very pretty. We'll sign up for listing as extras with all the companies, so we can work here on our days off, just like last summer. Pass around the reward flyers today, and ask after Mister Haines. Maybe he went into the movies," Ruth said. Every success seemed possible, even likely, in the clear morning air.

Mary remarked on the changes in course the ferryboat made at intervals, with shrieking whistles, and shouts from the captain and crew.

"They're dodging the shad fishermen and their nets and boats," explained Ruth. "This river teems with valuable fish. They even caught a big shark upriver recently."

"I thought the only sharks upriver were in the State House in Albany," joked Mary.

"Reminds me of Copley's painting of 'Watson and the Shark', you know, where he's helpless in the waves as the destroying jaws rush upon him from the dark water, and his friends try to pull him into the boat, while the sun lights up Morro Castle across Havana Harbor."

Mary shuddered.

"It's a dreadful image," she agreed. "What's that you're doing?" as Ruth worked a pencil stub upon a folded newspaper. "What does it say, 'Cross swords'?"

"Cross words. A new puzzle in the 'World'. What's a nine-letter name for 'a small falcon'? No? How about 'relative of a tramp'? Hoboken! Oh, New Jersey puns today. Seven letters, 'downwind of the stronghold'?" Ruth pondered.

"Fort Lee! And here we are," pronounced Mary.

The rumble of the steam engines somewhere below changed tempo as they neared the landing.

With the early morning crowd they surged off the ferry, avoiding automobiles, trucks, and freight wagons, and caught the streetcar heading up the Palisades Road, to arrive in the film community of Fort Lee, several city blocks of clustered warehouses, barns, and that four-story greenhouse that was the new Universal Studio.

"More, bigger studio buildings since last summer," observed Mary. "Everybody's getting into moving pictures. Lillian Russell divides her time between suffragette work and the silver screen. The paper says Geraldine Farrar will go West to film 'Carmen' with Cecil B. deMille."

"Well, I've read," said Ruth, "that she's leaving town because Arturo supports Italy joining the Allies' side against Austria, and of course, Geraldine was very close to one of Kaiser Wilhelm's family a while back."

Mary raised a disapproving eyebrow, but Ruth continued.

"Gerry and Arturo, several years now, but Toscanini wouldn't leave his wife for her, and went to Italy last week; his son has already gone over to sign up."

"Here's the Solax Studio. Look at the line already in front of Madame Alice's office."

* * *

Sunbeams staggered with the rising sun between Brooklyn's buildings across the East River when Raphael X. Neel joined the hundred or so longshoremen shuffling into a crescent facing the foreman for the morning 'shape' at Pier [16].

The foreman would pick thirty or forty men who might get a full day or more unloading United Fruit's big white-painted banana boat just docked from the West Indies and the Caribbean. The other men would wander back to the Longshoremen's Hall or a saloon, and try to look sharper tomorrow or at the next boat.

"Hey, boss!"

"You know me, boss!"

"Count on me, boss!" And more of the same until three dozen men received flat brass tags stamped with a number for the paymaster.

Raff noticed three or four Italians, several Scandinavians, some Irishmen, and a half-dozen black men, most locals he recognized. A checkerboard crew, as the Wobblies described a mixed-race workgang.

So, what's up with that, he thought, has Greasy Joe's labor racket pulled back from the wharfs? Maybe his contacts in the NYPD should hear about this, quick. Remember when the Gas House Gang went to pieces within days of Red Grogan getting the Roscoe.

And there was somebody else watching as the unchosen men dispersed. And didn't he look all hang-dog and disappointed, just like Raff was trying his best to appear?

"Hafiz."

"Mister Neel," he replied, as he accepted a torn postcard. "This scene, the ' shape', reminds me every time of that painting of the mass of workers, with two men and a woman with a baby, walking forward from the dark."

"Do you mean 'Quarto Stato', by Giuseppe Pellizza de Volpedo," asked Raff with a straight face.

"Real Populism, yes," affirmed Hafiz, and headed away from the waterfront to read: 'Meet me at L'Epicerie in Little Syria. French barque has a strange cargo'.

* * *

No alternative. Replace all the flame tubes on the two lower levels of Boilers One and Two, the pair he ran everyday just to keep heat and light aboard, keep the ship alive. Other boilers he'd drained the first month they'd docked; they were sound and ready to cook.

Would the Austrian owners pay to rebuild boilers in a ship trapped in a foreign port?

Two hundred German steamships and sailing ships of all sizes, were trapped in the sanctuary of neutral ports around the world, as were another fifty Austrian ships, and at least a dozen Turkish steamers. Twenty Nine German and Austrian ships bottled up here in New York. Thirty million dollars worth. He felt it like a personal loss. The British Navy operated squadrons in all the shipping lanes to snap up any merchantmen or passenger liners flying flags of the Mittelbund.

Chief Engineer Dargo Jarst picked up a wad of cotton waste and scrubbed the coal dust and grease from his hands, and took time to thank the oilers and wipers on their rounds, and while greeting the firemen shifting coal for the next watch, shared a rather ribald new joke in Slovakian with the Black Gang. Signing various inspection and maintenance logs, returning salutes and smiles. His engineers deserved formal compliments, especially with this week's potential for sport and chaos in port, so he wrote out notes, with carbons, for the main log, acknowledging the First and Third Engineers, and handed another, with personal thanks, to his Second, still on duty.

Deck officers might make a semblance of day and night while in port, but with steam up, the machinery must be tended 'round the clock; a long watch on the Hudson River for the last nine months, fourteen days, and…six hours. Think of the cost in coal to keep this ship from becoming a dead hulk.

Those dear British; need to remind them how much more expensive naval war could be, just trying to maintain the blockade of America and Europe…

His boots clattered along the metal grill catwalk above the heat- castles, auf English, bitte, he corrected himself, the boilers, and the engine machinery.

Off-watch, his dreams had taken him again walking down the middle of an impossibly long iron bathtub, then stepping out upon a balcony high above a wide, smooth river. That was pretty much his waking life at the Hudson Dock since sheltering here last August, though Herr Doctor Freud might call the corridor a repressed need to explore new opportunities.

Still, maybe one of his current projects would rattle some anchor chains. The Kah-und-Kah Marine, the Imperial and Royal Austro-Hungarian Fleet, could field no warships into the Atlantic, and the Pacific might as well be a private lake for the British, their Triple Entente, and the American republics. Oh, and don't forget Japan.

Now that British and French armies had occupied all Germany's colonies in Africa, and Japanese and Australians had walked onto all the German islands of the South Pacific there were no bases to support a German fleet. That should be the end of cruiser warfare, right?

Not a very good trade Kaiser Wilhelm made for part of Belgium and some Russian steppes, and no end to a War that looked more like vendetta or a blood feud, like dogs fighting to the death.

Still, look at German General von Lettow-Vorbeck, who refused to surrender, and inspires the nations with his back-country war in East Africa, threatening Belgian Congo and the French and British colonies with his army of Germans, local Askari recruits and their families.

Fifty trapped Austrian ships might constitute a hidden colony, as worth protecting as a distant province, he decided, as he bounded up the steep companionway to the bridge.

He gave greetings to the First Mate, and signed for a thick official letter from Consul von Nuber in Manhattan, arrived with the morning's mail at their box in the Post Office, just down the street.

"I'm to report before Ten," said Jarst, shaking the heavy embossed paper. Approval for my project, he thought.

"Hope they buy you lunch, Chief," suggested the Mate.

"See the log. Our French and British watchers are noisy today. Longshoremen, you know, Schaurmaennen, started a fight around four bells in front of Saloon Row. The waterfront's touchy, easy to stir up trouble. Two men on top of the Ferry terminal, sweeping our piers with big field glasses. Intimidating us or trying to provoke us; it's something new, be careful when you go ashore. Our deck watch will point out any lurkers."

* * *

In his narrow, sparsely-furnished office a couple streets away from Cass Gilbert's ornate new Custom House near the Battery, Captain Guy Gaunt regarded the framed rotogravure portrait of His Majesty, King George the Fifth, considered the maps of the Gallipoli beach-head where his countrymen still battered themselves against an unyielding Turkish Army, turned his thoughts to his wife separated from him by half the world, thought for a moment of another lady, and glanced again over the scattered reports sent in from all over North America by coded diplomatic telegram.

One name caught his eye. Charles Crowley. Offering to blow up our railroad tunnels in B.C. for a German consul out there in Seattle or San Francisco? Isn't that the name of that occultist-mountaineering chap living Mid-town?

No, he's Aleister Crowley. Writes for the New York magazines, including the pro-German ones. It's 'The Fatherland' that prints Crowley's exaggerated prose, no, what's that unfortunate new phrase?

'Over-the-top', yes. American readers would catch his mocking ridicule of the Kaiser's militarism and enlightened 'Kultur', but the German editor of 'Fatherland' didn't notice Crowley's sarcasm and was paying him good money to insult Germany. Good trick.

Captain Guy considered other propaganda issues his nation must address to the Americans. Persuasion, better word.

His Majesty's government negotiated loans with American banks to pay American industries and American workers to manufacture weapons, no, armaments, or maybe call it munitions, and food and supplies to be shipped to the Allies, whereas the skulking Germans and Austrians sought to organize work strikes, raise public opinion against selling weapons to warring nations.

All those Anarchists and Socialists who demanded better working conditions. Every time that haste or short-cuts in manufacturing caused waste or hurt a worker, let the workers be blamed. Who was that American who called them all 'paid minions of the murdering Germans'? Nice.

Try to sift this from the actual sabotage caused by enemy agents or anti-Capital Anarchists. Enough real sabotage to worry about. That fire at Roebling's New Jersey wire cable plant, where the fire alarms had been cut. Somebody dynamiting Cudahy's meat-packing plant out west the other day.

So many millions of subjects of Austria and Germany emigrated to work in the United States. Leave America's labor problems to America.

Now if we can just keep a lid on three hundred million Hindoos and their Ghadr rebellion. Some of their organizers right here in New York City, and all over the West Coast, too. Hire a few thugs, hah, the mercenary kind, not the devotees of goddess Kali. Maybe some recent rough work he'd ordered would slow up the Irish trouble-makers around here. His clerk, a former RN Rating, and reliable, knocked and entered.

"This bundle to the Post Office for today's early afternoon delivery, Huggins. The others go out with me."

"Sir," said Huggins, and departed.

And let's send a little encouragement for those Tin-Pan Alley boys. 'Don't Bite The Hand That's Feeding You' could have been written by Rockefeller or Frick, about foreign-born workers in U.S. factories, but the tune might catch on if vaudeville would take it, so print another edition of the sheet music, maybe press an extra five thousand discs at Columbia Records and distribute them.

Now: unrestricted submarine warfare!

The one weapon that could threaten the Royal Navy, and the blundering Huns were wasting their torpedoes on merchantmen and innocent passenger liners!

Even after a success like that of Weddigen in U-9, sinking three of our cruisers in an hour!

Just a month ago, a U-boat torpedoed the little liner 'Falaba', killing a hundred passengers, including an American, as they tried to launch lifeboats.

Why hadn't we promoted that story as another German atrocity? Old news now. When would such an opportunity come again?

True, the Germans couldn't get supplies from America through the British blockade. Best not remind the Americans of that trouble a century ago that started with a British blockade. And no need to remember the American Civil War, when British shipbuilders built and armed and crewed commerce raiders for the South's Confederacy, and swept American shipping from the seas!

No, best forgotten.

Gaunt ran through his mental list of contacts in Hoboken, where Germany's merchant fleet sheltered. Enough ships to be a threat, like the Kaiser's Imperial North Sea Fleet to the mind of a Naval officer trusted to worry about everything. Too many rumors were coming true, many of them from Jersey. Something bubbling there.

What about those waterfront rumours of saboteurs setting fire to our sugar cargoes with cigars? Can't be done, but get sugar hot enough and it will burn like tar. Better that we and the French and the Russians pass out rewards for information and co-operation. It's all American money loaned to us, anyway.

What was that poem of Kipling's, wondered Gaunt, as he considered the cigar he habitually held over the ash tray, avoiding piles of papers.

Oh, yes, from 'The Betrothed': 'a woman is only a woman, but a good cigar is a smoke.' Gods! the fellow should write ads for tobacco!

* * *

"They call me 'The Wolf of Wall Street' because I paid a couple of news-hounds to name me so in print, just as my good friend and rival, Mister Livermore, has been named 'The Cotton King', and recently, 'The Great Bear'. Whether you're a baseball player, a stock player, or a street-gang leader, a name and a reputation give you extra weight in a contest.[13]

"That's why you've come to me, Kaptain von Rintelen, or should I continue to call you 'Mister Hansen'?" Here David Lamar twitched his bushy moustache in a smile and winked a dark eye at the German naval officer, who held his frame, spare as it was, just off attention.

Von Rintelen waved a hand in a vague salute, "You know me from when I worked here on Wall Street for the big German banks before the War. My Prince...or I should say, my principals desire their monies to influence America's capital investment in armaments sold to the European War."[14]

"Yes, I hear you tried to buy a controlling interest in DuPont Powder. Can't be done; even before the war bucks boom, DuPont's net profits averaged eleven point five-seven per cent annually of invested capital; say, about five and a quarter million dollars a year. They may better that figure by ten-fold this year. Can you imagine?

"If your German diplomats could signal us before they start peace talks... well, the mere threat of Peace would cause a panic among the war hogs and you might buy any armaments makers you want at knocked-down prices," Lamar advised, shifting in his swivel chair.

"I see no danger of Peace breaking out," von Rintelen confided.

"Here's an approach: I'll hire people to spread rumors that the New York banks that sell French and British War Bonds are going insolvent, start a run among the small investors to make the banks look bad, hmm? No?

"What about bottlenecks in production of more specialized explosives, or chemicals…" Yeah, they'll call me 'The Chlorine King', Lamar thought to himself, remembering the dreadful news of poison gas use on the Western Front last week.

"My good friend Charlie Morse tried to corner markets, as when he raised the price of ice during this town's hottest summer not so many years ago; then he and Heintzie tried to corner copper, and started the Panic of 1907.

"No, let's look at how Edison and his competitor Bayer produce all of the chemical phenol, necessary for aspirin and explosive detonators. We won't overlook machine tools for turning shells, stampers for cartridges, grinders, cutting tools, the like."

"Ah," now Lamar was hitting his stride in smooth talk. "The crucial bottleneck in American production aiding Britain, France, and Russia, aside from the unlimited credit my nation provides them…Shipping, of course."

Von Rintelen's attention was held, and he let Lamar continue.

"Ship leases; building contracts; buy ships while they're still on the stocks. British and French shipping agents make constant efforts to get vessels into New York and our other ports to bring equipment, munitions, and food to their armies.

"You know your German merchant fleet sheltering in Hoboken, empty and rusting? Change their flags, lease 'em to your enemies.

"We offer your ships as leverage to get control of the hulls that carry munitions for your enemies, and you'll gain access to their offices, their schedules, their financial backers, hmm?"

"Ideal, for your intelligence services like Abteilung Sektion III, or 'Nachrichtendienst', what a great name, that last, eh? I know it translates to something like 'Information Collection' but it sounds so delightfully sinister.

"Let me contact Charlie Morse, he'll be eager for such a big shipping contract.

"Congress just passed last month the Seaman's Bill, which will protect sailors, not just on American ships, with improved safety and life-saving gear; but all foreign ships trading here must comply.

"Imagine a British ship that pays a crewman twenty-five dollars this month, comes back to the United States, and must pay that same sailor fifty bucks a month. Buy one of our faltering newspapers in Town here, and put the British to shame for exploiting cheap labor. Call upon President Wilson to sign that bill.

"We'll publish interviews, newspaper ads, billboards, telegrams.

Start a campaign with your emigrant countrymen here: 'Stop building weapons to murder fellow Germans'."

Von Rintelen picked up the thread. "Bribe Irish dockworkers here to strike when loading ammunition for the British Army."

"I have friends among the waterfront gangs like the Gophers, the Black Hand, and the River Rats. They influence the longshoremen, the teamsters, the warehouse and pier owners.

"I'll try to persuade Sam Gompers' American Federation of Labor to play ball, and the Big Union, the Industrial Workers of the World, you know, the Wobblies, the Socialists…

"If they won't play – oh, your money can set up a brand-new union, let's see, call it 'Labor's Peace and Prosperity', something like that."

Von Rintelen didn't quite follow. "How, please?"

"See, shipping prices go up, costing the Brits and the Russkies more, and your U-boat war's got to drive up shipping costs."

"Let me have that half-million dollars in your valise there; I'll put it to work organizing labor and public protests. Hmm, think I'll push the Women's Suffrage Movement to support Peace, yeah.

"To paraphrase your von Clausewitz: 'Economics is War by other means', eh?"

"Well," concluded von Rintelen, standing up. "I have critical machinery to buy up, and some intriguers to inspire all around New York City. Be sure to call on TransAtlantic Trust; I'll make German and Austrian funds available. Your commissions on these contracts should reward you."

They shook hands.

Out in the corridor, von Rintelen straightened his coat, and vaguely wished for a spare handkerchief with which to wipe his hand after shaking Lamar's.

He strolled down the carpeted hall of the big Manhattan Hotel to his next appointment, with the Great Usurper, Victoriano Huerta. Good!

Help him regain control of Mexico, challenge the United States' involvement there, ship German weapons into the country, deny Mexican petroleum to the British fleet, and build U-boat bases on both coasts.

For a while, Pancho Villa and Zapata held an uneasy balance with Carranza's Consitutionalists, but that broke down, and now word has come that General Obregon smashed Villa's Army of the North, partly with the help of machine guns, barbed wire, and German advisors. Time to stir up Revolution again in the United States' favorite neighbor.
If Sommerfeld and von Papen hate him for this, oh well.
And as for munitions: 'What I can't buy up, I'll blow up'.
Whee!

* * *

Raff found Hafiz in the back room of the French spice and grocery store, said nothing, but accepted the beer Hafiz handed him.

"You probably noticed the two Polish sailors who got picked at the shape," said Hafiz. "They're really German crew from the 'S.S. Wotan', tied up over in Hoboken."

"Thank you, I can use that." Raff figured Frank Tunney's Bomb Squad people should hear. "That barque up from Martinique; be a shame for it to catch fire with a hold full of sugar for the French army, eh? You see more with one eye than most folks do with two," Raff raised his voice, as the owner came in, smiling, to take up a labelled jar of dried herbs.

"Monsieur LeM-; well, doesn't matter, he employs eighteen detectives at Compagnie TransAtlantique, just to watch the hold men and longshoremen," explained Hafiz. "Something's getting by them.

You see anything out of the ordinary?"

"Everybody carries a weapon, here on the West Side wharfs, but you get caught with a sap or a shiv or a Roscoe, and 'Big Tim' Sullivan's law sends you up the River.

"So it's bale hooks," Raff continued, holding up a big tiger claw of steel, fixed cross-ways in a stout wooden handle, "a necessary implement for a longshoreman, or lead pipes, found everywhere.

"I've noticed so many more lead pipes in coat pockets than I used to see. More in the morning, than when the shifts quit in the afternoon, about yay long," he held his hands six or seven inches apart.

"Kinda short for a life preserver or sap," Hafiz figured.

"More cigar sized. Ties in with other things I hear. Could it be a plumber's smoke bomb, for testing pipes and vents?"

"Yeah, guards and detectives watch for items being taken out or stolen, rather than left behind," Hafiz looked at Raff, who nodded, as the same thought occurred to him.

Both men came to the same conclusion.

"We'd better pass this up the line," Raff decided. "Make sure you demand a good payment, so they know you're serious and not just blowing smoke, huh?"

"Damnedest thing. The English won't listen to advice from an Irishman, but they'll hear you," mused 'Hafiz' O'Connor.

"O' course," replied Raff, "New York City's hired a black policeman, so maybe my folk will have a voice, d'you think?"

They left the shop with other customers, and Hafiz made fake conversation.

"As I explained," he said as they passed, "I'm not really Persian, I'm a naturalized American from the Caliphate of Syria. One of Teddy Roosevelt's Hyphenated Americans."
Raff chuckled.

"Born in Mississippi, am I an American from the Hyphenate of Africa?"

Hafiz winked and shifted his eye-patch to his other eye. He thought it might be a good time to loiter as a shenango, looking for casual dock work, but I'll be practicing my old art of picking pockets, this time for lead, not cash.

* * *

In the Austro-Hungarian Consulate at 24 State Street, a taciturn sub-consul, Samuel Augyol, passed an envelope to Jarst and ushered him to the Consul-General's sumptious office, appointed with finely-woven silk carpets, lamps made from antique Chinese vases, and on the wall what Jarst took for an allegorical portrait by Klimt.

Alexander Nuber von Pereked waved Jarst to a comfortable chair close to his desk, and nodded to Augyol to stay. A lean nobleman in the prime of life, Nuber held up Jarst's recent letter in his thin, well-manicured hand.[5]

"Many sources report favorably on your experiences and successes with MarineEvidenz, so valuable to our Sovereign and our Navy, and your carefully-worded letter, suggesting an opportunity for innovative naval practices, intrigued me.

"A recent letter to President Wilson's Secretary of State, Mr. William Jennings Bryant, from Britain's Ambassador, directly accuses our Nation's merchant ships and those of Germany, of exactly the offenses against neutrality I believe you advocate here. Better to be hanged for a goat, as you point out. I'm entrusting you with everything you ask for: money, leave from the Naval Reserve, independent operation."

"Herr Augyol will give you all the papers, clearances, and the cash you need. Good Luck!"

And Nuber rose and shook hands.

* * *

Sidney Reilly shuffled several projects, and some Kings, Queens, and Knaves through his mind to help keep track of the face and allegiances his breakfast guests expected to see. Today it was a lean, swarthy face grim enough for Pluto or Satan, with the new style of thin moustache.[6]

Reilly stood up from the breakfast table, and from a cut-glass cruet he poured a stream of thick black oil into an empty orange juice glass.

"Oklahoma crude," he intoned, then dropped a handful of gold sovereigns, francs, eagles and rubles into a steel fingerbowl with a clatter.

His neighbor, the French Military attaché set a thin metal clip loaded with automatic pistol cartridges atop the gold coins, as he'd been asked, followed by the British Purchasing Agent, who covered it with a slice of buttered wheat toast, also as planned.

The assembled representatives of wartime purchasing seemed to appreciate his opening, and added silverware, linen napkins, and such, except for Count Florinsky, Russian sub-Consul and Purchasing Agent, who picked up a packet of sugar a couple of times, then set it aside.

Revealed, thought Reilly, and nodded to the British Purchasing Agent, while covertly studying Florinsky.

The French Military attaché, with contacts among the Sûrete, the Deuxième Bureau, and the Tsar's Okhrana, began speaking, and pointing to columns of American funds loaned to Europe's Allied Forces, as arranged on a poster.

"Look at the Eighty-five Million…"

At a previous conference, Count Florinsky had introduced his companion, Tamara Swinskaya, as a ballet dancer, and Reilly had determined to double the surveillance he'd set upon the Chairman of the Russian Supply Committee. More important, liquidate any of my remaining investments in the hopelessly corrupt Tsarist Russia.

The ballet dancer still lived in...not poor, but rather subdued housing in a boarding house frequented by vaudeville and show people. Reilly's search of her lodgings had turned up no jewels or other gifts, no bank books showing suspiciously-large additions.

No, an oaf like Florinsky could only keep Tamara's interest with information, such as the purchases and delivery schedule of American munitions companies to the Russian war machine.

This new German spy in New York: von Rintelen; had he set up this scheme, and would he produce more operatives to corrupt the war effort on American soil?[7]

Reilly thought it wouldn't hurt to present himself to the German spy, just as he'd done with others in German intelligence in America.

A bold approach could rattle their confidence, and might lead to a lucrative contract, based on his reputation.

Now, this other problem posed to him by the French occupied his mind, while the speaker enthusiastically explained the fortunes to be made with shipping leases, shipping insurance, and timely use of inside data. Florinsky wasn't the worst of this lot, he'd be fine.

Reilly contemplated the careers of German citizens prominent in New York, and knew personally of several bankers, not Germans, who assisted the Kaiser's agents here with funds legally and quietly moved through their banks, trust companies, or investment firms.

More alarming were the bank clerks, loan officers, and advisers who found employment in American or Allied banks, then used their access to report to the Nachrichtendienst on financing, even copying of documents dealing with shipments of weapons or war supplies, motors, chemicals, food, anything. Agents of Germany could report these figures through commercial channels with little danger of alerting Allied counter-espionage, let alone offending President Wilson's touchy neutrality policy.

There was a pile of money for everyone at the top, Reilly knew; less reward for the underlings, as usual.

The face of Paul Koenig seemed to loom large in Reilly's calculation of German influence: Chief of Police for the enormous Hamburg Amerika Line, so well represented in New York Harbor by the idle ships sheltering at the Hoboken Docks. American neutrality protected these ships from the fury of the prowling cruiser squadrons of France and Great Britain, but what if the vessels served as recruiting places for saboteurs, even arsenals of destruction, such as worried the French?

The Germans would pay to protect that secret.

Time to contact his people in New Jersey.

Funny, how more shadows could enlighten a subject.

* * *

Standing with Ruth in the lines of movie hopefuls, Mary thought about how the companies were moving away from the overbearing presence of the Motion Picture Patent Trust, to seek greater artistic, and needless to say, commercial freedom.

Mary knew the stories of hired thugs and saboteurs wrecking studios of the Independents, torching cans of film or burning entire buildings, rather than let the new industry freely develop experimental or unauthorized forms, or worse yet to the minds of the Patent Trust, low entertainment popular with the Masses.

Why not, thought Mary, idly watching her line of job applicants advance to the studio gate, any alchemy using sunlight to turn silver into gold will be jealously guarded.

* * *

The Great Beast of the Apocalypse awoke, leaving his night dreams of power and world domination. Throwing aside his bed covers, he patted the bare hip of his woman, then trod across the carpeted floor like a conquering general, no, an emperor of antiquity to inspect the new day.

Like a hero, he seized the thick curtains with both fists, thrusting them apart, as though they were the veil of a sacred temple fallen to his legions.

Yes, he exulted, Manhattan shall be mine also, if I apply my occult arts to my glory and to aid the success of British arms in that lesser conflict.

And those arts will help me raise some rent money.

Maybe better try to sell some of my book collection.

CHAPTER FOUR
Cliff-Hanger

Post Card

The Palisades, at Fort Lee, New Jersey
West side of Hudson River

Place
1 cent
stamp
here

Afternoon before Mary and Ruth finished their calls around Fort Lee, and they stood with others waiting at the ferry landing, reading or chatting. Mary heard that New York City was chasing out the movie producers, after some outrageous film crews made more than a nuisance of themselves by pushing their cameras into civic parades, weddings and funerals, neighborhood emergencies like fire; actors getting directly into these events, exploiting private functions for drama or comedy.

Mary thought some of these stories might be fabrications from supporters of the drawn-out lawsuit of the Patent Trust versus the Independent Producers.

Startled, by the terrible roar of a powerful engine, they looked up the face of the Palisades toward a squeal of brakes and rubber tires that couldn't hold the road.

A big racing-car howled out of control as a girl desperately reached for the brake lever, and the left front wheel dropped off the edge of the road, flinging the whole car on its side in a rush of crashing metal through shattering branches.

The runabout stopped, its exhaust still popping and drive chain rattling, barely held at the top of the cliff, by broken trees and brush, which threatened to collapse and drop the car and the girl off the dark, slick precipice.

"Oh, no, no," cried Mary, as everyone saw the white-clad figure of a girl cling desperately to the brake handle and wheel, all that could save her from falling to destruction on the rocks three hundred feet below.

CHAPTER FIVE
The Veiled Temptress

Then a cameraman on the edge of the rock shifted for a close-up, and a sturdy grip lifted the actress to safety, where she waved and bowed to her impromptu, cheering audience. Eventually, they could speak again.

"Was that Pearl White?"

"No, she's Upstate," said Ruth, "filming the new chapters of the 'Elaine' serial. The story where she's pursued by sinister Oriental villain Wu Fang."

"What? He's a perfect gentleman," exclaimed Mary. "He wrote about his visits as an Ambassador in America. I read his book last year."

Ruth just shrugged and waved her fan magazine.

They strolled aboard the ferry with other passengers, as a little electric van painted with advertising for a New Jersey dairy rattled and lurched onto the deck, followed by a dark closed sedan and an open-bed Ford truck. Mary and Ruth found benches by the tall windows amidships on the upper deck, the downriver side, which made Mary wonder how the operators called 'port' and 'starboard' on a double-ended ferry-boat sporting two pilot houses, and propellers at each end.

In any event, bells jangled down in the engine room to signal 'forward', and steam puffed out aloft as the ferry pulled into the River current, while Mary and Ruth discussed famous novels, plays, and authors in the movies. Other passengers filled seats near them, chatting. Mary was vaguely aware of two veiled women who had alighted from a dark sedan car before it drove aboard the ferry, and took seats against the varnished paneling opposite.

"Ofora- Muse of Fire, he named her, in the first line of 'Henry the Fifth'. Anymore, he'd be writing film treatments or directing one-reel comedies for Fatty and Mabel," stated Ruth.

"Who should portray her, this new Tenth Muse for the cinema, Geraldine or Theda?" asked Mary.

Ruth referred to her movie magazine.

"Mister Fox has signed Theda Bara for 'Carmen', and Geraldine Farrar will use her opera skills for a rival 'Carmen', directed by Cecil B. deMille."

"Two Carmens at once! What a fight! Geraldine's a great actress, but what use is her singing voice on the silence of the screen? I think Theda Bara would win: her slow, langourous style holds up to the over-cranked projection speed when theater managers try to squeeze in just one more showing every night," said Mary.

"How?"
"When the projectionist runs the film faster than life, most other actresses jump across the screen like electric weasels, and grimace like mad monkeys," Mary explained, "while Miss Bara seems to have a natural understanding of the mechanics of film projection."

"Her lazy grace, and thoughtful ease may be happy accidents, but Theda Bara's stately movements give the viewer time to read deliberate acting and expression.

"Mary, you should write for 'Modern Films'!" said Ruth.

"Of course, it doesn't help when the theater orchestra plays the 'William Tell Overture' during every romantic scene," finished Mary, laughing.

"And every theater manager thinks he can edit the film for his schedule, sometimes cutting out important scenes. No wonder people say moving pictures can't deal with serious subjects," suggested Ruth.

"But it's the cameraman, too, that cranks film past the camera lens at anywhere from 75 to 90 feet per minute; Billy Bitzer cranked the camera at 45 to 60 for 'Birth of a Nation'."

"Ugh," and Ruth gave a shudder. "Mister Griffith set movies back fifty years with that!"

"What do you mean? We've only had movies for twenty years," said Mary. "When was the first time we saw a movie, do you remember?"

"Five or six years ago when we visited Nova in Kansas City?"

"Three weeks back, the grain elevator people over in the next town projected some of Charlie Chaplin's and John Bunny's on the expanse of their white concrete siloes. The family I stayed with took our whole class over on their hay wagon."

After a while, Mary said, "I saw 'Cabiria' recently. The volcano exploding looks impressive, although I guess the story of the heroic African strongman, Machiste, who rescues the Roman, may have been propaganda for Italy's invasion of Libya, do you think?"

"At last Saturday's matinee, I saw 'Timid Mister Tootles' and another two-reeler, 'Mister Boobley's Baby', both issued this month," said Ruth, "I'd recommend them, but the prints have left local theaters for the film exchange, to be passed around the country until they wear out, like newspapers or magazines.

"Ephemera, mayflies, valued briefly by the fickle public, who looks for new entertainments, casting aside the used films for fresh images."

"Goodness, Ruth! Melancholy, from you."

"Yes, but the need for comedy or dramatic stories or adventure or romance never fades. The movies will be re-made with new people, new machinery, for new audiences," finished Ruth, looking at a bright, but fading, poster for a Mabel Normand movie almost two weeks old.

"We'll both write for the magazines," Mary decided.

As the ferry boat bumped to a halt, and the gates slowly creaked up, passengers pressed forward, eager to disembark. Ruth pulled out her watch.

"We can't possibly reach there by two, and it's too late to 'phone or send a telegram," Ruth said with dismay. "I don't know..."

Mary glanced to her right, at a quiet word of greeting, to see a veiled woman in black, pointing to an automobile near the gate.

"Ride with us across the Island, and across the Harlem River; I heard you must get to the Bronx Waterfront. We'll take you right to Mr. Lake's office without going out of our way, I assure you," she paused as recognition flashed across Mary's face, and holding up an imperious hand, continued, "Introductions after we reach the car, please."

In the spacious, closed sedan, Mary and Ruth turned to their hostess, who swept aside the traveler's hat and veil to reveal a pale, sweet face dominated by wide, world-weary eyes framed with dark tresses.

"Mary, Ruth, call me Theda, please. My sister Lori," as she waved a languid hand toward a younger woman with equal tresses of tumbling dark hair under a wide-brimmed hat.[8]

"We're both going by the surname 'Bara'. Forgive me dressing like Hetty Green, but I'm actually required by contract to be chaperoned and veiled in public."

"For her safety, and that of the public," said Lori. "You know: the threatening Sphinx and fierce Vampire, Man's Ruin, and Wife's Enemy?"

"Yes, as I trample Marriage under my careless sandals, ha-ha!... I prefer to think of myself as just Theodosia Goodman, a nice Jewish girl from Cincinnati.

"Our chauffeur will take us directly to your Bronx appointment, and Lori and I will go to meet Mister Walsh. Raoul says if we hurry, we can produce my 'Carmen' before Geraldine Farrar films her version in California."

"Don't worry, you've released three pictures already this year, and public opinion polls show that people prefer movie actors on screen, to screen appearances by theater stars," said Lori.[9]

Some talk about the industry, as the automobile crossed at Willis, and smoothly passed south on Grand. Theda was intrigued by Mary's middle name 'Bodacia' on her calling card, Ruth got over her attack of fannish awe in time to urge Theda to seek a role on stage or screen as a classical heroine like the British queen, or Zenobia, or the courtesan Empress, Theodosia of Byzantium. Theda looked pleased at the mention of her namesake, and Lori made a note.

"Here's One-Hundred-and-Thirty-Fourth Street, already," announced Lori. "See you this summer in Fort Lee."

Heart-felt thanks from Ruth and Mary, and they turned to the wharfs as the car of the Temptress drove onto the College Point ferryboat to cross a widening of the East River.

CHAPTER SIX
The Submarine Inventor

"You received this postcard in the mail, Miss Cowles?"

Simon Lake[10] turned his broad, confident face from the open window to smile under his big moustache at both women as they were ushered into the office by Lake's foreman.

"Yes, Mister Lake. With the Peoples' Line mail delivery on Saturday," said Ruth, and gave him a copy of the 'Reward for Information' flyer.

"Hmm, the message is only 'Simon Lake Submersibles' scrawled in pencil, addressed to you. The card is printed in Germany, and depicts Captain Weddigen's U-boat sinking British cruiser 'Aboukir' last year."

Lake looked doubtfully at her.

"Our sister's husband is missing. We would have ignored this card, but our inquiries have hit a dead end," continued Mary.

"Would someone want to dig me about German Navy infringements on my international patents? I can't see even Mister Holland's associates at Electric Boat doing that."

Lake wondered about the young women's motivations. Journalists? Or agents provocateur for a government? Doesn't matter. He must promote his submarine technology to all interests. Treat them politely, and practice for some important interviews coming up.

"Do you know I corresponded with Jules Verne? There's one of his letters, framed, on the wall."

"Wonderful," Mary and Ruth agreed.

"He applauded my use of submarines for salvage work and gathering marine resources."

Lake paused, frowning.

"I don't think he would be pleased at Germany's use of U-boats against passenger ships, though I hear they're launching a fleet of cargo Unterseebooten to run the British blockade and re-open trade with America. Again, infringing my submarine patents without compensation."

"Though how much patent protection can there be during a shootin' war?"

He studied the printed reward flyer.

"Your Mister Haines: I haven't encountered his name, but if he was assisting Irvin Gillis (he's a Commander in the United States Navy) to set up sales for Electric Boat to the Chinese, this could be a bad time for your brother-in-law to annoy the Japanese Military."

Lake picked up the day's 'Sun' from his desk.

"You've heard about the Twenty-One Demands, the Ultimatum Japan put to the Republic of China?"

"The other day, a very polite Japanese gentleman called on me here. He presented credentials as Matsumoto, of the Japanese War Materials Purchasing Commission, and very politely expressed his hope that Japan might acquire any of my submarines offered to foreign governments." Simon Lake shrugged, and gave Ruth and Mary a cautious look.

"Well, I guess I understand his very polite message. Japan hates the idea of China operating submarines. Imagine Japan's Navy and merchant fleet threatened by a vigorous submarine campaign like Germany' new U-boat war. I can't blame them for worrying."

Lake pointed out the window toward his salvage barge that looked like several steam plants and locomotives had been re-assembled to some purpose.

"Peaceful commercial uses of submarine technology salvaging a sunken barge. My crew walks downstairs through that huge pipe to an airlock at the bottom of the East River, gathers scattered pig iron bars, sending them up the escalator to our support ship.

"Valuable metal, but not compared to the two thousand bars of silver in the mud off Staten Island.

"Then, if you'll indulge me, we'll try to locate the wreck of HMS 'Hussar' sunk near here during the Revolutionary War, with a million in gold for paying British troops, and also, a hundred of our Patriots, who went down with the ship, chained up as prisoners."

Simon Lake handed the flyer and the mysterious postcard back to Ruth.

"So, whether the British would like me to leave it alone, or the Germans would like to stir up bad propaganda, I won't be dictated to by either."

Obviously the end of the interview, so Mary and Ruth thanked Simon Lake for his time, and departed, pondering the new political undercurrents swirling about their feet.

* * *

In his office at the Liberty Tower in Lower Manhattan, Vahan Cardashian frowned at the flimsy yellow telegram paper just handed him. From Constantinople (as he still secretly thought of Istanbul), it was not Imperial business for the Sultanate, so he set it aside and looked over the news reports from the San Francisco Exposition. Friendly comments in the California papers about the Turkish pavilion opening this week, and for the exhibits he had organized as Consul for the Sublime Porte.[11]

Good. That new phrase: 'public relations' occurred to him. Five million American guests would see the very best the Nation of Turkey could offer in Commerce and Culture.

Time to sign that Turkish sea captain's request for travel funds and equipment for his crew to perform at the Exposition. An itemized list, including 'flags, insignia, uniforms, cinema cameras, tickets for seventy-three men to San Francisco', and a lot of money.

Inspiration flashed. Give this captain, Kochab Reis, of the Turkish Naval Reserve, everything he asks and require him to make motion pictures of their trip and activities on the West Coast.

Hire a movie company to assemble promotional newsreels for viewing in American movie houses, and send copies back home for the growing cinema enthusiasm that had seized Turkey's populace, along with everyone else in the world.

Good promotion. He signed Kochab's request and wrote directions with the afternoon's mail.

Now this other thing, like a small dark cloud growing on the horizon. Forwarded to him from New York City's Armenian newspaper, 'Gotchnag', the telegram seemed filled with ugly words he remembered people speaking in whispers.

Massacre, expulsion.

The Government of the Committee for Union and Progress, the 'Young Turks', arresting Armenian bankers, clergy, and educators in the Capitol. Would it go as far as under the old Sultan?

Best to make swift inquiries about the safety of his sister and their aunt back there, if he wanted peace of mind to represent the Government.

Cardashian studied the large wall map of the Ottoman Empire Railways and reflected how the Turkish reverses fighting Russia, and the Army's failure to take the Suez Canal could move the ittihadists to desperate measures against subject nations like his own Armenian people.

An Armenian rising or British recruitment of an Armenian legion might spark a new round of reprisals or 'massacres' as the Europeans classed the sporadic tragedy of Armenia under the Ottomans.

God save us, he prayed.

The Wickedest Man In the World brought himself out of a light doze when an interesting conversation two seats up caught his attention.

"...all the talk about a 'Great White Hope' remember, Gonzalez?"

"Oh, yeah, the Big Fight in Havana three weeks ago," recalled Gonzalez.

"White slavery, you know, the Mann Act, 'transporting girls across State lines for immoral purposes', they formed a Bureau of Investigation in nineteen-oh-eight..." Squealing and grinding from the wheels as the streetcar turned a corner.

The louder man, who must be some kind of detective or police, explained.

"What I hear is the Federal agencies all want to be part of the protection of war munitions, maybe the big dog, so they're picking up contacts and informants."

"Trouble is, they don't all have money like Treasury or War, or the big companies, so they're making threats to Socialists, Anarchists, Populists, Unions, gangs, tongs, small business, trying to put the squeeze in, like our friends in the P.D."

"I gatcha, Mack, maybe I'll see you Saturday at Union Park. The May Day parade. Point out interesting people, not just the Suffragettes."

Gonzalez stood up and descended at the next corner; the loud detective, three blocks later.

Well, I wonder who they were talking to, thought Aleister Crowley.[12] I might not be the only important person aboard. Oh, really, now, what am I thinking!

* * *

They found an inexpensive seat on a ferry back to Manhattan, and as they passed the foot of East 25th Street, Mary pointed out Arbuckle's Ship Hotel for Girls.

"I wish we could board aboard, like our first summer out here," said Mary. "They would sail the whole vessel and all the tenants over to Coney Island for an afternoon."

"It's too far from our office, and they're threatening to close and scuttle the 'Jacob A. Stamler' this year," said Ruth. "All the working girls aboard will scramble to find new quarters…Won't take much and we could all face hard times, like the poor girls in O. Henry's stories; they're real cases he met or read about, you know."

"I could sell magazines and newspapers on the corner, a newspaper carrier; I'd be a regular Tabloid Mary."

"Don't joke. They caught Mary Malone again last month, working in a restaurant; she'd only infected a few diners. They've locked her up on Randall's Island; we rode right by there."

"I wouldn't mind being located in the Martha Washington Hotel on Twenty-ninth; they've a program exclusively for young working women, too. And Women's Suffrage Headquarters."

"Mmhmm. We'll return to the office, but let's go to a new place on Spring Street . They'll make us a pizza pie; gotta try it. Then drop in at the Jiu-jitsu Club on Broadway, and see about continuing our lessons this summer."

* * *

Chief Engineer Jarst returned to his ship, the 'Martha Washington', aboard a tugboat pushing a barge of coal, paid off the tug's master in cash, then signed the logbook with his nom de guerre, for which he carried a new passport issued by the government of His Imperial and Royal Majesty Franz Josef, Emperor of Austria and King of Hungary.

The passport was dated 1914, and bore several entries appropriate for a commercial mariner. It wouldn't insult American neutrality at any likely encounter with their inspectors, but Jarst held no illusions about fooling British naval intelligence. Word was that some haughty British Foreign Office people pushed themselves into the American State Department's Committee meetings for examining foreign passports, and were dictating policies for the United States now, so they could block the passage of enemy citizens and Reservists like himself.

Two crewmen, both armed with automatic pistols, had accompanied Karst back to the ship, where he locked away in the Captain's safe an attaché case stuffed with packs of U.S. Greenbacks, Austrian hundred-kronen notes, and large-denomination British banknotes.`

A meeting with the Old Man, who knew Karst's marine intelligence connections, gained Karst co-operation of the deck officers and crew for the most visible part of this project, since it involved the blessing and written approval of the local representative of the Austrian government in New York, Consul-General Alexander Nuber.

He based his plan on the desperation of the owners of Austro-Americana Lines to find money to cover the terrific costs of their empty ships and unemployed crews, and sure enough, the Board had telegraphed approval for repairs on their idle ships and permission to negotiate contracts to transport cargo.

They might even agree to lease or sell valuable ships that faced rusting away or being sunk by French or British warships. The Line trusted their experienced Captains to protect these tremendous assets. Someone else paying the bill made the proposal irresistible.

Unlike a man-of-war, say, Germany's cruiser 'Prinz Eitel', interned for the duration of the war at Newport News, a port of the neutral United States, 'Martha Washington', and the other Austrian merchant ships were merely sheltering, and could legally leave port any time they paid their port fees, and, of course, dared to risk the attention of British and French cruiser squadrons.

A call from the watch brought Karst to the wharf side, where a big Mack truck rumbled to a stop, and the driver brought up a clipboard with receipts and bills of lading to be signed. Karst had already paid by certified checks from his Manhattan bank for these items, and turned over the stowage duties to the First Mate and his deckhands.

Several large crates broadly marked 'electrical equipment' and 'wireless components', 'Fragile!', 'Do Not Drop', presently sat on the forward well deck. Karst mentioned the fine weather, and that there was no great rush to stow these crates below. He overcame the urge to survey the neighborhood of the Dock for the inevitable watchers.

Hope they get an eyeful, he thought.

Karst expected a foreign agent or a hired detective would have established a listening post or even tapped the 'phone lines of the small office he rented upstairs of Bohack's Grocery in Brooklyn, though it contained little more than an empty desk and a telephone set.

He didn't mind being heard talking to the Masters of other Austrian ships in Boston, and the Chesapeake ports, where substantial sums of welcome money for ships and crews were already arriving with bank messengers.

Several captains had agreed to wait at shipping offices for scheduled phone calls.

On the surface, Karst planned to ready the ships for sea, and load them with cargoes of scarce strategic materials, as though ready for a mass break-out of blockade runners to evade the British blockade. Nothing to offend U.S. Neutrality, as long as these maneuvers involved commerce and not battle preparations.

But the British could not ignore it. Forty-six thousand dollars scattered to eight vessels would establish a pattern, and make the Allies worry about the other idle enemy ships that could be readied for mischief.

Prepare the ships for sea with a great show of expense and industry, not just filling with fuel and supplies and cargo, but with the legal paperwork to clear the ports and operate in lawful trading capacity. The Austrian Government had missed an opportunity to protest the tightening of the British blockade of all Northern Europe, following an indifferent and silent German leadership. A blockade of reprisal was contrary to international law.

Last week, Jarst had signed contracts and paid deposits for three different firms of Marine Ispectors to tour and then write reports on maintenance, hull integrity, and sea-worthiness of all Austro-Americana ships in New York harbor, copies to be submitted to the Company's underwriters of insurance.

That would draw the attention of British naval intelligence. Karst meant for them to anticipate a mass sale of an idle fleet, to operate under neutral flags.

Or worse, a mass sally, a break-out of blockade-runners, to re-supply the Mittelbund with critical materials. A nightmare for Navies straining to operate warships on expensive patrols.

Jarst saw the tangled knots of Naval Strategy, not so much a lack of battleships and cruisers for Germany and Austria-Hungary to challenge the British fleet, as a lack of support bases.

Look at Admiral von Spee's fleet, beating the British cruisers at Coronel, but meeting destruction at the Falklands, crippled by no coaling bases. Germany's loss of overseas ports in Africa and around the Pacific in the first days of the War made their deployment of large warships impossible.

A second option to naval warfare: submarines. Not nearly enough of them to seriously interrupt Britain's shipping, nor to develop tactics beyond the lone wolf raider deployment practiced by U-boat captains.

Karst saw a third option, a ship vaguely forming in his mind, as though advancing out of a fog...

But for now, best to go ahead with 'Sun-tzu' this week, and let the newest concept develop as it might.

* * *

"Mary, that was Paul Lettridge, at the New York and Cuba Mail Line office. He's found William Haines' name," and here Ruth paused to let the news sink in. "On the passenger list of 'S.S. Morro Castle', for the first voyage this month to Havana, Cuba. No listing of his name on any returning ships, but we'll receive the printed lists in this afternoon's mail delivery."

"Puts us back in the search," agreed Mary. "We can call the local offices of the other Cuba lines. But let's send Mr. Lettridge something nice for his prompt discovery.

"Something like a deli basket, or, I know! We walked by the Life-Saver Candy plant on the West Side yesterday as we distributed flyers and collected signatures for Votes for Women. We can send him a box with a sincere note of thanks by pneumatic tube, and he can have it within the hour. If ... oh, dear, when we locate Billy Haines, we'll give Mister Lettridge something more."

Mary leaned against the wall, pulled out a long crimson-wrapped package of Mikado Imperials Number 4, tore aside the wrapper depicting the new Emperor of Japan, a vermillion sash emblazoned with the Order of the Chrysanthemum crossing his navy-blue uniform coat, and shook one of them out.

Mary scratched a short match with her thumbnail, as she'd observed the cowboys do, applied the flame to one end of the Imperial to soften the resins. She took in Ruth's skeptical look.

"It's something I learned from the Kansas cowboys, who all smoke."

She stubbed out the match in an ash tray, set the pencil into the cast-iron sharpener and ground down a keen point and shook off the cedar shavings.

"The Japanese can make a ceremony of preparations for the most humble activity. I think it's a good idea, concentrating one's thoughts.

I'll finish the requisition forms; we can type them up for the Captain's approval first thing in the morning."

* * *

In deep leather-upholstered easy chairs that didn't so much rest on the thick, antique silk carpet as grip it with claws carved into the wooden feet, five plutocrats smoked good Latakia tobacco rolled in Manhattan machines tended by the same hard-working women who had recently rolled cigars by hand.

The eldest of the five remarked, "The Second International is collapsing. M. Jaures' assassin made a better shot than Princep."

He continued. "This War is breaking the international Socialist momentum, which would have carried the World in another generation."

His neighbor chuckled.

"Reading Werner Sombart and Max Weber, again?"

"It's the Unions we need to manage. I can calculate a percentage of Union membership where this country would be lost to us," said another, who paid less attention to his new chorus-girl wife than a man his age should.

"If we conscript all our workers into an Army of National Defense, that'll reverse the Wobblies' advance."

"Reverse IWW is, what, WWI?" quipped the youngest.
And the fifth, who remembered his grandfathers had been Patroons in the Valley, spoke up.

"Replace the workers' zeal with Nationalism, promote racial hatred, show the World real Schrecklichkeit and Terrorism aimed at everyone, instead of bullets and bombs just for the Bosses, teach the young men and women they won't inherit any more of the Earth than a trench, either in Belgium, or in Ludlow, Colorado."

"Oh, John, you make it sound too easy. Where's the sport in taking the wealth of the world from people who are afraid and starving? Have a drink, or you'll be closing the saloons next. Then how will anyone know how to vote!"

And the group fell to laughter, before seeking their cars and beds.

CHAPTER SEVEN
On The Elevated

"The Captain is hiring cooks for the Summer season on the boat, consulting with the Chief Steward, and they will both want to know what kind of bandsmen and musicians we locate; the Captain has final approval. I think he got a good response from the guests about the 'Liberian Liners' we brought in last year as late season replacements. Let's try to sign them again," suggested Ruth.

"OK, then we need some attendants, for each bathroom. Restroom supplies, new chamberpots for the cabins; and cleaning and maintenance will be organized by the Chief Steward. Who is he hiring on as stewards this year?" Mary said. "He'll have to buy fresh flowers at each landing."

"Captain hasn't posted names yet. And the Captain will personally arrange for armed bank messengers, but we'll give them access to the safe at both ends of the run."

"The Company's contracted for newspaper advertising, they started in March, and they'll really begin promoting excursions the first of May," mentioned Ruth. "The stewards will order all linens and dining ware. The cooks will organize their own shopping for dining guests and mess crew…I think we're done. Leave all these with the Captain's office staff Upstairs, he's across the River at the Jersey machine shops until late this afternoon."

"Lunch," decided Mary.

At the deli, the counterman who claimed to have invented it, served them a grilled hot sandwich of thin-sliced pastrami, melted Swiss cheese on rye bread slathered with thousand island dressing, and loaded with steaming sauer-kraut. Pickle on the side.

"I'll get one of these again," affirmed Mary, finishing off her coffee.

"Told you you'd like it," said Ruth.

Riding over on the trolley to connect to the 'L', they discussed how to advance 'Votes For Women' in the current campaign.

"...and spend our afternoons canvassing our assigned neighborhoods. Six hundred thousand families in this City, and somebody has to bring the message to them."

"'Votes For Women' will only happen if we commit to informing and persuading citizens at the personal and family levels," agreed Mary. "Isn't New York the most populous State? Success here will sweep the Nation."

Ruth nodded.

"We're gaining ground with the labor unions, all the immigrant support societies, shopkeepers and small employers, and progress among the big money. Saturday will be May Day, and we may find ways to help petition-signing with the parades around Union Square. Here's the Nineth Avenue Elevated station."

Trudging up three long flights of stairs to the Elevated station seemed even harder in the warm afternoon sun. One step after another, thought Mary, is that thirty-nine steps? A train of three cars roared in, and squealed to a stop. Mary and Ruth gratefully sat down facing forward, about halfway back in the middle car, and idly noted the social mix of men and women before them.

Mary thought that this one sitting on the lengthwise bench appeared to be too well dressed to be a teacher or office manager, maybe a stockbroker or banker with his expensive tailored clothes, paperwork bulging out of his flat leather case setting next to him on the brown cloth padded seat cushions.

Directly across the car, facing the man Mary thought of as a rather self-satisfied banker, sat a thick-set man wearing no hat and starting to bald, dressed in loose clothes, with a dark cloak around his shoulders, even on such a hot day. He gave Mary the impression of a poet or artist, and she could imagine him sketching mysterious black-clad figures in Gothic settings.

Two men sat down between Mary and the banker, on forward-facing seats as the train started North again; looked like Eastern European transplants, judging by their simple clothes, clean celluloid collars, cheap hats: maybe employed at some small offices.

The cars growled Uptown, and the artist fellow, whose thick, expressive hands matched his shaven head, seemed to direct his gaze at the banker, who started to nod off, eyelids sagging shut.

Was the dark-clad poet muttering some chant, thought Mary, herself feeling a little drowsy in the afternoon sun. Is he working something in his hands? Some criminals used chloroform to rob or attack. Could she smell pungent, dangerous fumes that would dull her mind?

Just then, the train halted.

One of the office clerks rose smoothly, leaned over the benchback, neatly lifted the bulging briefcase from the seat next to the banker and without haste, moved for the exit.

Blatant theft rowsed Mary, and she shrieked.

"Thief! Thief!"

Mary jumped to her feet, pointing.

"Stop making a scene, Mary," said Ruth.

"He's stealing that case! Thief!"

The banker was now alert to his loss, and trying to scramble after the thief, but the second clerk had surged to his feet, and stumbled forward, into the open door.

As the pursuit moved onto the platform, Mary was aware of the dark-clad man moving for the exit, and glaring at her with hatred and wrath in his wide, staring eyes.

The train pulled away, and the other passengers looked with amazement at the lightning-fast disturbance, so quickly finished and taken from their sight, as pursuers raced down the Elevated stairs, desperately trying to catch the thief, who had gained a passing streetcar.

Mary tried to contain her anger and disgust at such bold daylight robbery upon a public conveyance, but she was shaken, and not just by the heavy cars rumbling through the switches.

"Let's make a policy," she told Ruth, when she could speak, "to carry only a small purse we can tuck in our coats, and not extra baggage, if we can."

Half a mile behind her, Doktor Heinrich Albert stopped chasing the trolley, lowered his frantic arms, and with a shock realized the loss of German government documents, which he had been delivering for safe-keeping to the German consulate.

These documents outlined the use of Imperial funds to buy influence and opinion in the United States, and some illegal, even warlike actions were discussed. It's alright; he consoled himself; they're all in the German language, but they should be retrieved before the thief thought to show them, or sell them. Maybe advertise in the local newspapers, offer a small cash reward to catch the attention of the thief before the case left New York City's underworld.

If the sleepwalkers in America's government read such a frank discussion of Germany's contempt for a neutral nation,...well, best start immediately to mend losses.

He trotted off to find a taxi.[14]

* * *

Chief Engineer Jarst didn't trust wastebaskets, and he felt uncomfortable with so many loose letters, telegrams, and financial statements lying about on the desks at the Austro-Hungarian Consulate in Manhattan.

Since he'd begun his secret plotting, he was more concerned with, and aware of the many threats to secrecy and security in a foreign city filled with the enemies of his Sovereign.

An officer of the Imperial and Royal Navy relied on his subordinates to assist in the technicalities of operating and sailing a ship, so Jarst was necessarily fluent in more than the required four languages of the Empire, besides German, commonly spoken in the Navy.

He was, of course, aware of the separatist and nationalist aspirations of some the Empire's peoples (just look at how the Serbian nationalists had fired the first shot of this War).

Jarst wouldn't presume to criticize the Bohemian or Slovak workers handling Consular business in a great financial center like New York City, but the presence of his country's enemies working so near in offices all around Town, even in the same building, determined him to leave no papers concerning his secret plans when he left the Consulate offices.

And the British were watching him, as evidenced by some missing cobwebs in his Brooklyn office, and some papers that weren't crumpled quite as he'd left them in the wastebasket.

* * *

"Here's West Twenty-Eighth Street, the famous 'Tin Pan Alley'," shouted the conductor of the passing two-decker sight-seeing bus through his megaphone.

"Look, you might see Irving Berlin, composer of 'Alexander's Rag-Time Band', Scott Joplin peddling a new Rag; oh, listen they're playing 'Cotton Boll Rag' upstairs there..."

Ragtime, just what I need right now, thought Mary; could be blues, I suppose, riffling through the petition book Ruth handed her. Never have learned a musical instrument; there was that magazine ad of Geraldine Farrar, the opera star, listening to a cabinet Victrola; maybe they could buy one on time.

Imagine walking down both sides of one city block; then imagine stepping inside every business, shop, basement, main door, and how many steps needed to visit every apartment door on each side of poorly-lit, cluttered hallways on each side of every floor of the four-, five-, six-, or seven-storied apartment buildings. Don't call them 'tenements', the word now carries a taint, and these are people's homes.

They'd finished another block of canvassing, collecting signatures and addresses, wearing long purple ribbons, wide as cartridge belts, across their shoulders, 'Votes For Women' printed in block yellow letters.

Every storefront, walk-down restaurant, fruit stand, delicatessen and street level cafe or coffee shop (avoid the saloons, because the gin and liquor and beer dealers associated Women's Suffrage with the 'dry' and temperance ladies, obviously enemies to their livelihood), then into the apartment doors to the offices, small manufacturing, social halls, schools and church offices, not neglecting the walk-ups, cold-water flats, and tenement rooms going up five or six stories.

"Take my clipboard while I carry these buckets upstairs for Mrs. Murphy," said Ruth, as they ascended, with weary tread. Had the pipes to the upper floors failed? A smile and a helping hand brought 'Votes For Women' closer. Wouldn't do to look like a snob, or some superior-minded reformer; this is for everybody.

Then, next door.

"Five stories on this building. Standard 'dumb-bell' shape," gasped Mary. Seventeen more steps to the fifth floor. "Wider front and back than the middle, creating narrow air shafts between buildings. Allows fresh air and light to the back of each flat." Theoretically, she thought.

"I usually recite the words of a hymn," said Ruth. "Just now I was keeping step with 'Bringing In The Sheaves'. Otherwise, it's 'Onward, Christian Soldiers," or the 'Temperance Battle Hymn'. I dearly love 'Whispering Hope', but it won't get me to the top of the stairs."

Strategies recommended by the Committee had them start at the top floor, so rumor of police raids or criminal shakedowns, let alone visits by an unwelcome landlord, would not cause all doors to be shut fast. Mary and Ruth had taken blocks primarily occupied by English speakers, so their standard opening was a brisk knock, light, non-threatening, followed by:
"Votes for Women! Please sign to help get the vote in November."

The petition pad would be held forth, along with sharpened pencils of the purple indelible dye that could not be rubbed out. Mary had suggested this improvement, knowing the value of indelible pencils for postcards that must be handled and passed around.

Conversations and explanations helped to make the visit feel like a social call. Now and then Ruth or Mary would provide a stamped tin stick pin with the slogan (each carried a small bag full of pins they purchased themselves), and they considered it a triumph when a woman or a man would accept a card so they might get involved with the movement.

Back downstairs, and on the sidewalk, Mary looked up at the top of the building opposite them.

"That one's built in 1898. See the little block with a carved date, nestled under the cornice below the roof line?"

"Oh, yes. Is there a name for that architectural feature?"

Mary shrugged, not remembering any name.

"Well, big civic buildings have their construction date on a corner stone, so maybe that's a cornice stone?"

"Good enough for me."

All of a long afternoon, until nearly sundown, they spent canvassing one street. How many blocks in the West Side, in Greater New York?'

Six hundred and sixty-one thousand registered voters in town; they haven't all made up their minds, and their families may influence them.

If the heat wave stayed away tomorrow, maybe they could get in another afternoon for the Cause, after work.

A tall gaunt Englishmen, and the equally tall Prussian dandy with boyish good looks, who might have been rival naval attachés ignoring each other, both smiled to see Ruth and Mary pass on their way home, while curb traders still frantically waved call slips to potential customers, and concealed representatives for the Great Political Powers, as well as the Business Lords, scurried about the maze of New York City.

* * *

Jarst acted as agent for Austro-Americana Lines and called upon the Port Inspector's Office, making a big show of paying off port fees, accruing every day since last August. He filed the billowing piles of papers without which modern ships were truly becalmed, received official signatures and necessary bureaucratic stamps, handed in maritime inspection and insurance forms necessary for departure, and rounded up copies of forms to be filled out by each ship's Master for clearance from the port, including cargo manifests registered as food such as sugar, butter, packed meat, certain strategic materials like rubber and tin and copper, but no, repeat, no munitions, weapons or explosives.

All shipments were consigned to warehouses and established merchants in Rotterdam, in the neutral country of Netherlands.

Britain already claims Hollanders buy too much sugar and rubber and meat for their own use, and must be selling cargoes to blockaded Germany right next door, and the Nederlanders respond, "How dare you try to ration our food!"

Jarst didn't bother to leave any spoiled or incomplete copies behind; a good spy system, or its paid investigators should be able to borrow or rent papers they needed to see.

Today, get the new wireless receivers warmed up and staffed. His radio officer was training competent men who could listen, keep careful records of certain wavelengths and frequencies used by the British Navy along America's Eastern Seaboard.

His crew already listened to the airwaves to catch changes in messages from Belize, Bermuda, and Newfoundland. Even though they couldn't read British code, increases in traffic might indicate nervousness, or an irritability of the British Lion's hide.

If the British fleet made a show of force around New York Harbor while the American Fleet prepared for Fleet Week and the Presidential visit in early May, a propaganda incident could draw America's attention to dangerous maneuvers, in and around U.S, waters. Look at the concern caused by Japan's cruiser stuck on a reef in California, with the Imperial fleet gathering to salvage the ship!

Jarst understood he must not offend American Neutrality by warlike acts operating from American ports; America will side with Britain, since their banks have loaned fifty billion to the British government for the War, but he would have to see how far he could twist the Lion's tail, waste Royal Navy resources, and start Americans taking a new look at their British friends.

Make the Lion look foolish, and win!

He went over the plot in his head, as he rode west across the Hudson River on the coal barge pushed by a tug.

First Three Days: start maintenance and re-provisioning of 'Martha Washington' and other trapped Austrian ships.

Hire several tug boats on charter to keep steam up on all watches, ready for the big departure. They needn't sit idle, but could buzz about moving barges with piles of bulky cargo back and forth between Austrian ships. Call all marooned crewmen back at full pay.

Second Three Days: stack bags of coal on deck, and lash those big bundles of railway timbers wrapped in cable against the wheelhouse, as though for protection against steel splinters thrown by shelling.

With extra sooty cheap coal, some of that nice soft brown limonite (Ammonite? No, lignite!) from Montana, get steam up, and alert New Yorkers of the life returning to hopeless, stranded ships, in all the involved Austrian merchant ships.

Seventh or Eighth Day: The Ambassador and the diplomatic staff will protest the illegal British blockade, and notify the press of the coming break-out, the intention to defy, and run the blockade, and restore free trade with Europe.

Invite press aboard, not screening out British agents, to observe preparations.

Covertly call in Austrian Naval Reservists stranded in America, for full pay aboard the blockade runners. Foreign agents would notice.

Announce excursion boats to observe the pursuit of the blockade runners by Royal Navy warships. New Yorkers would swarm to rubberneck at a sea battle right off Coney Island.

"Hurry, Hurry, Hurry! Be present at the greatest Atlantic battle of the Twentieth Century! See latest newsreels of British Navy attack on helpless merchantmen, right off our shore!"

Ha! Fast boats with photographers and motion picture cameras to record the gruesome spectacle. Remind the Americans of the nearby British war fleet prowling like a lion, seeking whom it could devour.

Circulate a story that the first ship to clear port would send off her crew with the pilot boat, and be remotely-controlled by radio from another ship for the rest of the voyage, as a humanitarian effort to preserve seamen's lives from panicky British salvoes of gunfire.

Show the press a wireless device rigged to the steam-powered steering gear in the stern of a merchantman, and a big wireless repeater, although a little study would convince a steady mind that such a voyage was impossible, except maybe for a Diesel-powered vessel.

Maritime law would shudder at the idea of a basically derelict vessel under way through the shipping lanes without a soul aboard. A legal, as well as a technical impossibility. So, don't show them boiler rooms and coal bunkers still arranged only for men's labor.

And on the Seventh Day, if monitors show increased radio traffic, assume the Brits anticipate a mass break-out of valuable prize-ships for their cruisers dispersed along the American coast. More warships steaming fast and expensively from their bases in Jamaica, Bahamas, and Canada.

Then, wham! Cancel the whole kerfuffle, bank the fires in the boiler room, pay and shore leave for the crews, dismiss the tugboats, while the French admirals have to pray they can coax tired old cruiser hulls and machinery back to the Windward Islands. Remember the Ile d' Martinique, and St. Pierre City, before the volcano? Ah!

Two days pass, and suddenly black coal smoke belches from the idle merchant ships again. Getting closer to Navy Week in New York City.

British radio traffic again fills the ether, the British destroyers and French cruisers again struggle to take station to control approaches to American ports.

American authorities listen to furious Allied diplomatic protests, citing obvious preparations to supply German warships, in violation of neutral nations forbidden to serve as bases for belligerent warships.

This time, it shuts down the same day, and the clean, active Austrian ships are offered for sale, while somebody like the British Naval Attaché, sitting in his spider-web of tripwires and alarm cords, adds up the cost of this exercise on the Allied fleet: expenditures of bunker oil, coal, wear on machinery and crew, and general cost to alertness with two false alarms, crying wolf.

This is going to work, he exulted.

All the food cargoes aboard would be donated to New York's poor, publicly, maybe through the Relief Agencies and Settlement Houses.

As the barge approached 'Martha Washington', Jarst observed parties of sailors setting extra electric lights around the masts and rigging of the ship for overnight work.

Several large stages hung along the sides, with work crews scraping rust, then priming and re-painting the thick lead paint the 'Martha Washington' had slowly shed, like a corroding wet-cell battery, while idle in port since the previous summer.

Jarst smiled to himself. A few Austrian ships sheltered in ports of the southern United States. He'd read of Civil War blockade runners who defied Federal gunships, and were regarded as heroes, at least by the rebelling States. He wondered, did the American public remember the American Civil War?

CHAPTER EIGHT
China Town

Around lower Broadway, Japanese industry diverse as Kawasaki Shipbuilders and the Yokohama Specie Bank, the Jiu-jitsu Club, and Morimura Brothers Nippon Dolls, present the best of that nation's efforts to the world concentrated in New York City.

At 8:48 on Wednesday morning, April the Twenty-eighth, two middle-aged Chinese men in dark conservative suits entered the lobby of the Yokohama Specie Bank.

"Seven," said one to the starter, who rattled castenets in his hand to signal the elevator operator, who was already pulling the folding cage open and reaching for a grip lever big enough to drive a locomotive. Studying the wide black directory board that listed offices and occupants in white letters, a youth, also Chinese, and wearing a good, if inexpensive suit, held a light student's cap as he scribbled in pencil on a postcard, then turned away and left the building.

From the front desk, Matsumoto Jotaro nodded to the American detective reading a tightly-folded newspaper, who settled a round bowler hat on his head and slipped outside in time to see the student pass a picture postcard to a well-dressed gentleman lounging behind the wheel of a shiny runabout idling at the curbside.

The detective looked up and down Broadway, as though seeking a taxi or streetcar; the gentleman drove south, gears whining as he merged into traffic. Hand signals were subtly given to tail the Chinese student. No need to follow Lieutenant-Commander Dudley Wright Knox, U.S. Naval College, and probably Office of Naval Intelligence.

The hired detective reported back to Matsumoto, whose duties to the Empire of Japan included bank examiner, Manhattan sub-consul, and operative for the Navy Police, the Tokkeitai.

Matsumoto recognized this little drama as a social call, part of the diplomatic tango, communicating without clumsy words.

Ever since January, when Japan challenged the shaky new Chinese Republic with Twenty-One Demands, (uncomfortably echoing the Austrian Ultimatum upon Serbia just before War broke out in Europe) the United States had understood the warning for America contained in Japan's message to China: 'Stop loaning money to Chinese mines in Manchuria, hands off the Cheffoo and Wu Chang Railroads, and you'd damn well better block Bethlehem Steel from building that Fukien naval base for China'.

Feelings were even more touchy, since Imperial Cruiser 'Asama' ran aground in Lower California, and the massive salvage efforts by other Japanese ships sparked wild rumors of a Japanese invasion. Poor 'Asama', named after the active volcano, currently erupting again, he'd heard. So far, only Mister Hearst's newspapers promoted this panic.

The local detective agency would keep U.S. officials informed of all the efforts on behalf of the Japanese Government, to avoid unpleasant surprises or misunderstandings, and everyone assumed that the detectives would sell the information to other interested parties; the clients must expect double-dealing from mere hirelings. Everyone hoped that the dance wouldn't come to resemble that of the Apaches in Paris.

Nevertheless, fifteen minutes later, in Chinatown, Li Lian noticed her cousin Li Yong walking rapidly. He doesn't see the two highbinders shadowing him and closing in, observed the slight high school student, as she gripped her papers and book bag tighter, held her blue-flowered cloth cap firmly over her long hair, separated from the sidewalk throng and skipped across Mott Street, dodging jitney cars, electric taxis, and delivery trucks rattling their chains as drivers slammed big shift levers into place.

Lian recognized her cousin's stalkers as well-known hatchetmen for the Hip Song Tong. Wouldn't do to break the tenuous peace between the local benevolent societies. Lian felt it best not to call out, so she just stepped up faster to fall in and take the arm of Li Yong, who didn't even start with surprise.

"Good morning, Cousin Lian. You don't know how happy I am to have company. Uncle's shop is just down the block," said the young man with a tense smile to her, then kept his attention straight ahead, not glancing at their countrymen, who were dropping back.

Vendors shouting from their pushcarts, traffic horns, and the general roar of the morning street seemed to dismiss any potential trouble walking through China-Town.

An interminable two-minute walk brought them to 'Han Import', where Uncle Fon himself stepped out, took Cousin Yong's hand, greeted Li Lian loudly, and led them briskly off the street into a narrow high-walled shop lit brightly with bulbs shining through painted silk shades and jade-green prisms. Li Lian noticed Uncle Fon now had short hair, though he kept his long moustache.

Then quickly past a shimmering bead curtain and a heavy door to a cramped back room. Five Chinese elders, who resembled some of the Eight Immortals, but dressed in Western clothes, sat around a low square table and made no greeting but nods. Li Lian knew them as councilors for the On Leong Tong of the China-Town businessmen. Li Yong spoke to them in low, respectful tones, reported what he'd seen, bowed, and was dismissed to other errands.

Uncle Fon turned to Li Lian and gave her a wide grin.

"So much trouble you helped my nephew past. He followed a couple of General Yuan's men to a meeting in the Japanese consulate. They've been all over Town this week seeking help for the usurper.

"Now, one shadow trailing Li Yong back here would have been enough to see where he went, but two meant danger for him, maybe an ugly message for all of us. So clever of you to notice, and brave to intervene. Ask me for anything!"

"Pleased to help, Uncle, and may I be so bold as to ask for your signature on the New York 'Votes For Women' petition?"

Fon laughed out loud, and signed the top sheet of the offered pad.

"Long live America! Long live the Republic of China, and confusion to the Warlords!"

The councilors echoed Fon's cheer with enthusiasm and reached for the petition, although one was heard to mutter, "And an early repeal to The Chinese Exclusion Act." After introductions and more thanks were made, Uncle Fon led Li Lian out a side entrance to a waiting taxi, and handed the driver a five-dollar bill.

"One of our people, niece. And here's a note to your teachers that you've been taking part in current civics issues. We hope to persuade our friends in the other tongs to join our boycott of Japanese goods, and to openly support Sun Yat-Sen's republic, rather than the usurping tyrant."

* * *

Wednesday morning raced for Mary and Ruth as they met with the Captain and the Chief Steward, prepared requisition forms, order sheets, pay vouchures, and a dozen other instruments to make the excursions sail smoothly for Manhattan's citizens who would seek relief from the summer's heat out on the River.

With the day's business complete, Ruth covered her typewriter, Mary finished filing, and they looked to spend the afternoon on errands, business with personal, and with their political pursuits.

Next door to the Jiu-jitsu Club, Mary and Ruth went in to the Kyoto Tea Room and Curios for tea and noodles.

"You won't order basashi again, Mary," teased Ruth.

"Please! I just asked about it that one time." Mary didn't continue, having trouble folding her umbrella, still damp from showers earlier on the street.

The Japanese hostess helped them hang their coats by the entrance, and set their umbrellas in a stand by the door, then led the sisters to a table, halfway back in the room, which was decorated with bright printed silk hangings and painted screens to break up the space and give some privacy to the scattered patrons.

A tea tray arrived instantly, presented by a girl wearing a costume of blue and white cotton that owed much to traditional geisha clothing. With a smile, the server set out the tea articles, took their orders for noodles, and departed.

In mere moments, she returned with plates on a tray, also loaded with covered porcelain dishes of steaming noodles in a light ginger sauce.

"Just exactly the right nourishment for a drizzly afternoon," affirmed Mary, as they set to eating, and turned to their map and canvassing assignments.

"And the nerve of that critic to compare Theresa Bernstein's new painting 'Suffragette Rally' to 'Stag Night at Sharkey's'!"

"The prize fight picture? Yes, both show violent, untamed passion. So what's wrong with that?" Ruth wondered.

During a discussion of canvassing tactics and efficient block-walking patterns, a clattering noise from the front startled them. A couple of minutes later, the hostess appeared at their table, her face all apologies.

"Please, I'm so sorry, ladies, a gentleman tipped over our umbrella stand, while retrieving his cane. He wasn't hurt, but I fear for the umbrellas you left there."

The hostess was not re-assured by the storm cloud that gathered on Mary's face.

"Please let us pay for your refreshments today, and please accept a replacement parasol, of the best new Japanese design, for I would be ashamed to send you out-of-doors without rain protection," and she gestured through the front window, where earlier clouds had not entirely vanished.

At the cash register, Ruth picked up her venerable black umbrella with the white celluloid handle, and found it had sustained no injury. Mary's had taken a severe kink, and wouldn't open again, so she yielded to the hostess' apology and accepted a parasol with a sturdy steel shaft, and ribs covered by heavy silk painted in glorious colorful patterns. Mary made sure to pay for their meal, insisting no alarm or inconvenience was incurred.

Once on the sidewalk again, Mary opened the parasol to find the waterproofed silk bore brilliant colors that positively glowed in the returning sunlight, so even Ruth was impressed.

"Beautiful printing; clouds of purple butterflies passing below the Rising Sun at Fujiyama, the Sacred Volcano," pronounced Ruth admiringly. "Spring steel construction, and what's that strange carved handle?"

Mary held it out.

"It's heavy cast-iron, covered with orange lacquer. Seems to depict a grotesque little horned devil, with tusks or fangs, and holding a knobby iron war-club."

"The whole item feels suitable as a weapon, capable of serious blows. Hmm," considered Ruth. "Let's make the other stops on our list before we go back to canvassing for 'Votes For Women'."

* * *

"Mary, did you notice the sharp look we got from the clerk there when we gave him the advertisement copy for the 'personal' section?" asked Ruth as they walked down Williams Street towards the trolley stop at the corner.

"And he excused himself, to take the copy back to the editor's office.

It was another five minutes before he finished and gave us change for the run in this week's issue," answered Mary. "I had the distinct feeling that hidden watchers had been alerted to look us over."

"Yes, remember, 'Gaelic-American' is the voice of the Irish Republican Brotherhood, John Devoy's revolutionary group. They raise funds and organize public opinion to support Ireland's separation from Great Britain," explained Ruth. "The 'Tribune' last month reported someone carrying German money to buy surplus rifles to arm the rebels in Ireland and India."

"That won't sit well with their British overlords, will it?" said Mary.

"Let's run up to that trolley as though we're going to jump on, and see if anybody reacts."

"Yes, I think we might be followed," said Ruth when they stepped back from the trolley car. "I caught a glimpse of a bowler I recognize as a standard Burns model."

"And the burly oaf in the straw skimmer. Pinkerton? No one else would wear a straw hat before season."

In fact, twenty-one eyes closely watched the progress of the Cowles sisters across town, as they switched from trolley line to foot, then caught random jitneys to lead shadows a merrier course.

A Japanese office clerk pointedly ignored the glare of the hatchetman from the On Leong, while a Russian immigrant in thrall to the Okhrana narrowly stepped back to avoid treading on the heels of the plain-clothes New York Police Detective, right behind Carranza's operative working for the Nachrichtendienst Sektion 3.

The girl of the Lady Gorillas gang curb-crawling in the silent electric brougham, the camorraista from the Mafia Black Hand, and the college student in the Serbian Black Hand might be reporting to anyone, guessed Hafiz, as he dropped out of the parade to send his own reports to Pinkertons, Burns, the British naval attaché, and the United States Treasury Department. He felt vaguely disappointed not to spot a French presence, maybe Inspector Lecoq, or Fantômas, for example.

* * *

"I was impressed how those Pinkertons stayed across the street from Burns' people when we transferred at the last streetcars," said Mary.

"Don't be fooled," advised Ruth. "If we spotted those that stand out like missionary teams, be sure they had an inconspicuous tail we wouldn't notice, maybe among the clerks or shopgirls heading home.

"Mary, if those Pinkertons and Burns and Police detectives shadow us, it will make our slipping in and out of apartment buildings and businesses harder without attracting suspicion," said Ruth. "What about the secondary shadows, the ones we don't even notice. And I can't stop thinking about bandits, blowing chloroform under our door at night, like the white slavers."

"Don't worry; although chloroform has been reliably reported in the papers as a weapon of attack; use has gone way down since Mad Doctor Mors escaped custody.

"Story about another attack with chloroform, heard it from a neighbor, who heard it from a relative, who heard it at church; not very firm, you know.

"Anyway, the criminals piped chloroform vapor over the door's open transom, thinking they'd be able to rob at leisure. But it turned out the residents were absent and had left a gas light burning, so when the fumes touched the open flame, well, the thugs were elevated to a higher plane of existence," finished Mary.

"Oh," gasped Ruth, laughing. "I doubt if it really happened, too!"

CHAPTER NINE
Pestilence

Right across Buttermilk Channel from Governors Island, where batteries of ten-inch guns defend Upper New York Harbor, in an old decaying house that matched his blighted mind, the original 'Horror of Red Hook' abandoned sanity to make an ally of what was nothing but an enemy, reached for the jar of anthrax culture, and packed his germ weapons into glass tubes ready to spread disease in the town.

He was hired by a native-born American who burned with zeal to support the war of ancestral Germany, had traveled there, and let himself be convinced he should carry germ cultures back to America.

He already had a target, where transients kept too close company to resist contagious bacilli. They might die, but only after they'd taken transport elsewhere, and the spreading pestilence would break the efforts of the enemies of Kaiser Wilhelm.

CHAPTER TEN
Orange Oni

With all her office work and orders set, and Thursday free until a late-morning meeting with the Captain and the Chief Steward, and Ruth meeting with bank clerks concerning her duties as Purser aboard the excursion trips, Mary Cowles spent a couple of hours in the Reading Room of the New York Public Library to research Japanese art.

The meetings, and piles more of office preparation for the season, took them late into the afternoon.

"Twenty cartons of souvenir postcards of the ship and the River, arrived from Union News Company," reported Mary. "They'll print more and deliver with two days' notice during the summer."

"No time for canvassing for the cause this evening," said Ruth, "so let's try for a few hours tomorrow afternoon, Friday. Then, Saturday, May the First, is Moving Day here in New York, as many people's leases run out; we'll ask Headquarters if they recommend canvassing for that day."

"I dropped off our petition forms, and picked up fresh pads, when I went to the Library," reported Mary.

"Oh, yes. Strangest thing. Western Union delivered a telegram at the office. Look here," said Ruth, passing over the thin paper form. "I gave the telegraph boy a dime, but right after he left, a Yachtsman-type wandered into the office; you may have seen him get into his limousine as you returned; dressed like a country-clubber, looking for his Aunt Sophie, and wound up asking, no, demanding my home 'phone number. So I told him 'Edison 5470'!"

"Oh, Ruth, you didn't! Why not just the old 'High Bridge One-Two-Three, Jump?" Mary laughed, and unfolded the telegram, and showed it to Ruth.

The telegram said that Lieutenant-Commander Dudley Wright Knox would call upon Mary at her office before six in the afternoon to view a valuable acquisition he hoped he might purchase.

"Too many words; easier to just 'phone." Ruth voiced her suspicion, Clock says six now, I don't think the gentleman is going to appear."

"I think he already did. That country-clubber Yachtman you talked to. He was looking for something. Surveying this office."

"I believe this message is to delay us. Let's call a cab, right now, and get home," Ruth insisted. "I've a suspicion what they're after, and I don't want to be out if somebody's watching us."

Mary agreed without dispute.

In the privacy of their own room, after meeting Mrs. Markowitz in the front hall and giving her news on the campaign for 'Votes For Women', they hung up their coats and Ruth picked up the parasol they had both started to regard with unease.

"I thought so," she said, twisting the decorative iron grip. "It unscrews!"

"Maybe a hidden sword blade, no the shaft is solid, but the figurine is hollow: is that a roll of microfilm? No, just a slip of paper with the same Japanese characters as on the label pasted inside the parasol. Oh, well," Ruth sounded disappointed. "What is this strange little Japanese devil, all teeth and horns and talons, clutching a metal club like a baseball bat?"

"He's called an 'oni'," said Mary. "I looked it up in a library book on oriental art."

"How do you spell that?"

"O,N,I."

"ONI. Does that represent something?

"Just a fierce folklore creature, I suppose," answered Mary.

"I wonder why it's colored orange."

Ruth considered this.

"I thought there'd be a secret message. I wonder…"

At that moment, a knock on the door startled them, but Ma Markowitz handed Mary a telegram she said had just been delivered to the front door.

Opened, the telegram offered one hundred dollars, to be wired immediately, if Mary would sell her new Japanese parasol to Captain Martin, at the Holland House Hotel in West Forty-second Street. Please reply this address.

"Uh, oh," said Ruth.

"I think the first telegram, at the office, was genuine, from a real person..." Ruth paused, to form a thought, and went on, "so this one is a ruse, maybe sent by that phony country-clubber to lure you into danger."

"Dacoits, Ruth? And I saw that recent movie by Tod Browning, 'The Highbinders', where the Tongs went to war. Filmed right here with some of the actual participants," said Mary.

"No, the Japanese government might hire anybody local," decided Ruth. "I hope William Haines didn't fall in with one of these Powers."

"We won't stir from the house again till morning."

* * *

Jarst felt like tearing up the letter he'd just received Special Delivery by a U.S. Post Office motorcyclist who drove up to the gangway of the 'Martha Washington'.

Paul Koenig, Hamburg-Amerika Chief of Police for their Hoboken Docks, on advice from von Rintelen and von Papen, and confirmed by German Ambassador von Bernstorff, required Austrian personnel to cease and desist alarming preparations aboard Austrian vessels on Eastern Seaboard of United States. Just like that.

Later, he felt even worse when Consul von Nuber's telegram informed him that Austro-Hungarian Ambassador Dumba ordered that their German friends and allies must not be 'upset'. Reading between the lines, Jarst thought the original word may have been 'defied'. Grinding his teeth didn't help. Friends and allies; oh yes.

Von Nuber included a further note, "See me tomorrow A.M."

The patron saints of Mariners, including Saint Brendan and Saint Elmo, must understand the need for a good string of curses.

Should he go ashore for a drink, maybe find a fight, or help Second Engineer Preissen rewind the armatures in the emergency dynamo? He chose the work.

* * *

Sundown's last rays flashed on the manure fork Raff pitched cleaning the temporary stables in Van Cortlandt Park in the North Bronx. Kinda outside Raff territory, but he'd pick up a half-dollar the rest of the night, plus all the stories his eyes and ears could catch.

Let's just shuffle over by the incoming chutes, he figured; that's where he heard the professional with the Maryland drawl was recruiting stable hands for some obscure mischief.

Sure enough, there was a pale skinny gent addressing stable hands finished with their day shift.

"I'm called Doctor Delmar, New York Veterinary Board," he said, holding up a shiny badge, "and I need to vaccinate all these mules for glanders and anthrax, before they mingle with other horses and cattle being shipped to Europe. Healthy animals will make a difference to the British Army."

Raff could see the Doctor handing out silver dollars and little, what, cigars? No, get in closer, those are glass test tubes with sharpened wires thrust through the rubber stoppers. Why doesn't he have some staff people with him?

"Time is short. Stick them in the shoulder or neck, then dip the needle back in the safe and in-active liquid, then stick the next mule.

Another dollar every time you empty a tube and bring it back for another."

Raff watched for a couple minutes, then stepped up and collected his dollar and a tube. A wary distrust made him drift toward the other side of the mule pen.

Oh, man, that's just wrong. He noticed the other hands didn't work any too hard to poke the animals, so maybe other people had doubts.

He stepped among the chutes, and faded past the fences into the gathering night. Somebody downtown needs to look at this culture. He thought uneasily of Typhoid Mary or Doctor Mors the Hospital Poisoner.

Some time later, Raff found a phone booth, asked 'Central' to connect him with Rector 8012. The switchboard operator in the Equitable building rang an office, and a voice spoke flatly, "Purchasing". Raff knew this was part of the British War Supplies Purchasing Mission, and one of the things they purchased was information.[15]

* * *

Charles Dana Gibson let go of his girl's arm long enough to shake hands with George Herriman, joshing, "You're the real Crazy Cat, man," as Irene Langhorne Gibson shook her flowing hair and handed petition sheets to Ashcan Schoolgirls May and Florence. They canvassed the banquet hall filled with a mostly male crowd of writers and artists for signatures in the New York Votes for Women campaign, with complete success.

Joseph Clement Coll rattled a fountain pen against a teapot and called this week's meeting of the AtlantInks to order.

"The lamb chops are Keen's Special tonight," he recommended.

"Announcements: Nell Brinkley's bringing Robert Frost to the next meeting, along with Windsor and 'Gertie the Dinosaur', and Plum promises to stop misquoting Keats and Shelley." Scattered cheers and laughter.

"There's Bert Williams, Bert – did you bring guests from the Frogs tonight?"

The tall, dark entertainer from the West Indies turned down his mouth, winked, and moaned, "Nobody," to general delight and applause.

While Marcel Duchamp performed a grotesque jig, jerking his elbows and knees until the company recognized 'Nude Descending' with loud shouts, the Great Beast of the Apocalypse smirked, signed the attendance roster, adding a Cabbalistic sigil, then passed the clipboard to Hugh Lofting, who signed, and with a few swift strokes, sketched a flying parrot.

Hearst's baseball writer Damon Runyon, from the other Manhattan, shook dice for his companions, saying, "It is never to be thought that I would deceive you, just ask my friend Nathan from Detroit, and I may solemnly advise you to cherish 'Don't Pass' as a steady comfort in a time of trouble."

His friends Kriemborg and Wodehouse stared at each other, 'in wild surmise', while they listened to comedian Bert Williams relate droll personal sketches from the filming of his new picture, then tell the story of how Hafiz the Persian Irishman had been blacklisted from the big vaudeville circuits.

"'It's how he's a booking agent; he snooped for a couple of the Big Mushrooms like Keith and Albee to find out how much their acts had to spend for rent and supporting their families, so the management would offer no more than necessary.

"Then they found out Hafiz booked himself to small houses in between the big circuit stops, which saved him going broke on rail fare, something too many of us have known. Decided Hafiz was either disloyal to their management or too tricky, so they blacklisted him. But Hafiz knows everybody. Now he's a pretty tough agent."

"Strangest thing," mused Wodehouse, as his turn came up for story-telling, "Our neighbor's daughter, Roberta, an impatient and strong-willed college girl, has accepted a marriage proposal from young Elwood; you've met him; that totally in-offensive and self-effacing youth. She previously despised him as a weakling. He enjoyed some shocking experience recently that opened his eyes, I'm told. If I can't get the rest of it, I'll have to run it up as a short magazine story; call it 'Elrod's Electrical Séance', hmm?"

Dan Goodman, the scenario writer, stood up in front and gave an inspiring tribute to John Bunny, buried earlier in the week, "In every way, the best and biggest man in moving pictures and comedy."

Frederick Mordaunt Hall, who also wrote about moving pictures in the 'New York Journal', when he wasn't advising the British Admiralty, came back in from a telephone call, nodded to his guest, and they made their way to a back door.

Their closed sedan slipped out the alley, eased quickly through light traffic across the Bridge to drop them at a darkened warehouse on the Brooklyn Docks, where another car was waiting, and watched as Raff handed over a dangerous package in an open door to William Gleaves, Royal Navy.

Raff knew little about Gleaves, a black man from Canada, except that he held rank in the British Naval Intelligence Division, conferred regularly with rich and powerful men, and might expect to rise with the success of his nation, in contrast to Raff's situation.

All the more reason to work for his advancement, and same applies to me, thought Raff. Well, dumping his old Nineteenth-Century birth-name of 'Jackson' for a new moniker should focus his identity.

Gleaves took the test tube, wrapped in an old sock and stuffed in a lead pipe, in his hand protected by a thin surgical glove, and set it gently into a cigar box, well padded inside. He closed it with thick rubber bands and set it into a sturdy leather attaché case, with pads to keep it upright. Another man brought up a bottle of carbolic acid solution and insisted on everyone rinsing their hands.

"We'll burn your old clothes, once you change inside the door. Not the thing for needless chances," said Aleister Crowley.

The balding, thick-set Englishman with the staring, challenging eyes passed Raff a new suit of blue serge, too large, but good quality. Now here's someone who could cast the Evil Eye, thought Raff.

All precautions finished, Gleaves waved the new-comers forward from their cars. Raff noticed a Welshman he knew to be high up in the Cunard Line's dock police, and a taciturn gentleman in evening dress who probably spent more time in a naval uniform. They listened to Raff recount his earlier work in the Bronx.

And there was Raff, Raphael X. Neel, gambler, hustler, rag picker, longshoreman and part-time agent for four police forces, three companies, and six World Powers. 'And a few years from now, lawyer and advocate,' Raff told himself, making his report of his observations in the Bronx to the shadowy figures by their limousines.

"Where the devil were the guards?"

"At the gates, and patrolling the outside of the corrals, so nobody steals any horses, I expect," explained an American voice.

Edward Karr, his thoughts centered on the horses and livestock he moved for the Pennsylvania Railroad, on their way to France, handed Raff a leather wallet that clinked in a charming, golden way.

"Don't go up there again, Mister Neel. I think the New York Police squads and some detectives will be thick on the grounds after tonight," said William Gleaves. "If you help us catch this Marylander, we'll have more of that for you."

No time for games. Raff told them quickly how he had spent a brisk hour shadowing the Needle Doctor, as he thought of him, to a derelict house in Red Hook, then turned aside to telephone William Gleaves.

After three words, "I followed him..." Captain Gaunt held up his hand, turned to Karr, and said, "We'll take it from here," nodding the American back to his limousine. Gleaves motioned to Raff.

"Captain wants you along."

Gaunt gave orders, "We'll take my car, Huggins will drive. Mister Neel as guide; Mister Crowley for issues of hygiene and science; pick up two Lascars who trained as wrestlers, and whom I trust, at Pier Eleven. I've extra pistols, and Mister Gleaves, I know you are never without necessary burglary tools."

Ten minutes, a fast drive, streets empty except for delivery trucks, a careful halt in an alley off Van Brunt, Raff with the West Indian, Gaunt leading the Lascars. Gleaves studied the dark house for lights, plied his jimmies and lockpicks, and they advanced.

But the Needle Doctor[16] was already fled, spooked worse than the animals he'd attacked, taking most of his apparatus with him.

In the kitchen, Aleister Crowley collected jars, suspicious test tubes and glassware and Petri dishes, small cartons, and items that might contain pestilence or addresses, or any other evidence, packed them away in heavy rubber bags, clamped them shut. He recommended they touch nothing and leave quickly, then clean up at a nearby refuge, or safe house. He advised the Lascars, Mehmut and Akbar, in their own language that they had all been exposed to unclean things, and that they would be well recompensed for the danger and pollution.

Crowley determined to move up the date for his visit to the great pharmaceutical companies in the Midwest. Can't wait, now. Later, he must write some detective stories dealing in a discreet way with tonight's adventure.

Gaunt realized he'd have to pass a careful word, and some money to local health officials. That house couldn't be left alone, unguarded, but neither did he want anything like a suspicious fire to alert friends of this Needle Doctor. Time to start reviewing the literature for similar ideas, and most of all, keep it secret.

After this night's work, Raff figured His Majesty's Royal Navy could spare a few more coins drifting to the National Association for the Advancement of Colored People, and if some pounds sterling helped the International Workers of the World, and the organizing of the new Agricultural Worker's Council, well. Best to keep hustling.

Sleep in his hidden garret was interrupted before dawn by images of microscopic disease bacilli magnified in curved glass tubes, until he rolled over and found better dreams of the Jungle Princess.

CHAPTER ELEVEN
On The Sharp Edges Of The Night

Jarst accepted the glass of Viennese wine handed him by sub-consul Augyar, and stood at attention in his Engineering dress grays as Alexander Nuber von Pereked proposed the health of Emperor Franz Josef. Glass recharged, he drank to the success, just announced today, of Austria's submarine U-5 and her crew, commanded by George von Trapp, sinking the French cruiser 'Leon Gambetta' in the Adriatic Sea.

For the third toast, Consul-General Nuber personally re-filled Jarst's glass, and pronounced, "To the success of His Imperial and Royal Navy, and that of our Ally, as we carry the Flags into new waters!"

Nuber then shook Jarst's hand, saying, "You may not take the capable Austrian officers you requested; the Germans disapprove, and are watching us more closely than the Britishers. Instead, you will carry out your third plan, without German knowledge, commanded by an officer from one of our other allied Navies. He's on his way upstairs now."

Jarst didn't wonder at his head spinning a little.

* * *

"Here are the incoming and departing mail steamers at New York," said Ruth, holding up a handful of newspaper clippings.

"We'll study them later," suggested Mary. "Right now, it's receipts, pay vouchers – enter and file, advertising flyers for the office to mail, tickets, lunch tickets, claim tickets – examine and re-box for storage on board 'C.W. Morse'.

"Oh, and the release forms for people putting their automobiles aboard, for use at the other end of the voyage, North or South."

Hours of necessary preparation for the rapidly-approaching season lasted until just before lunchtime.

Today Mary and Ruth took luncheon with the Captain and officers and senior staff aboard the paddle steamer 'C.W. Morse', using fine crystal and porcelain dining sets in the elegant dining room astern on the main deck, where the guests could enjoy river scenery, watching through the large windows that surrounded the room. The cooks tried out stoves and other equipment in real working conditions, trying out their teamwork with the serving staff, while the stewards made sure they could serve salads, steaks, fish, vegetables, soups, and desserts, either a la carte or d'hote.

Serve New Yorkers a good meal under holiday settings, and make them repeat customers, maybe several times a summer. Word-of-mouth advertising could not be duplicated, so help the voyagers promote the Holiday on the River to their neighbors and co-workers.

Then it was across Town and across the Bridge.

United Fruit, Munson Lines, and Cuba Mail all held offices in an enormous structure of warehouses, shops, and commercial spaces called the Fulton Store, stretching half-a-mile along the East River south of the Bridge.

Mary and Ruth found no difficulty picking up fresh copies of passenger lists from recent voyages carrying mail, passengers, freight, and fresh fruit for the tremendous U.S. Eastern Seaboard markets.

Helpful and efficient clerks and ticket agents provided handfuls of printed folders listing all passengers' names and home cities for all the sailings in April.

Most lines operated weekly, even twice-weekly sailings between New York and Havana, San Juan, and ports in Mexico, Venezuela, and Columbia.

Most Americans didn't bother with passports when traveling the Caribbean routes, so no State Department lists would show comings and goings. Customs and Treasury lists would be a long shot, and they'd decided to forego those.

"Peoples' Line? Hudson Navigation? Please have a seat." Only one clerk looked askance at Mary's and Ruth's employment, asking, "Charlie Morse coming after Ward Line again?" After that they stuck to their sister's story and kept it personal, instead of commercial.

Mary had no time to study the list to find William Haines' name as they walked between offices facing the Port of Greater New York.

They caught an open trolley to take them South on Furman, then Columbia, between the roar of trucks, locomotives and rail traffic, and the equally loud East River, filled with ferries, tugs and lighters, freighters, and occasional warships from the Navy Yard.

"This is our last stop today. All of New York and Puerto Rico Steamship Lines' passenger lists for April, through today," said Ruth as they rode on Court Street north towards the Bridge. "We can study lists when we get home. Or stop for a meal on the Lower East Side?"

"We're a long way from home, with many transfers and too much walking," calculated Mary.

Back across the Brooklyn Bridge and into Manhattan, Ruth paused at the next mailbox to drop in a couple of postcards, although to stop, or even slow down in these crowds, was like wading against a strong river current.

She was aware of more than just thousands of people moving up and down the streets at the end of a work day.

"His last message to Nova was a postcard."

Mary gave a disdainful shrug of her shoulder.

"William Haines? Oh, yes. You're referring to 'The Man Who Would Not Work'. You realize Mister Haines has probably just run off and left Nova."

"Sordid, but not unheard of," said Ruth as they stepped off another trolley. "Yes, I never thought he was much account. But we'll exhaust our inquiries before we have to console Nova."

"I think we're being followed again."

"Yep," said Ruth. "I haven't spotted 'em yet."

At the next mailbox, Mary flourished a post card a little more than necessary, pulling down the cast-iron flap, then letting it bang shut.

Maybe a Teuton on the corner, and that Italian fruit vendor with the pushcart was using his eyes a lot more than his gestures or voice.

It was in the next block.

"Watch out!" Ruth's voice snarled, and her eyes flashed sharper than her hatpin, jabbed through the hand of a rough-dressed vagrant grabbing at her bag.

With an oath, the ruffian stumbled to a tenement stairwell below sidewalk level, and plucked the six inches of stiff steel wire from his right hand, threw the stinging weapon down the steps, then waved his good hand to his partner across the street.

"Imagine! In broad daylight on West Fourteenth Street," Mary gasped. No, it's getting late on a Friday afternoon, the neighborhood doesn't look so quaint and charming all of a sudden, she thought.

We should have stayed on the trolley, gone farther Uptown on it.

Doormen urged the crowds of passers-by to step into the bright lights of the music hall lobby, buy tickets for the on-going show.

Song poured out of the vaudeville door:
"...and if Turkey takes a stand,
they'll get Ghurka'd
and Japanned, and you won't sing
'Hoch der Kaiser' anymore!"

The roaring chorus faded as they walked down the block.

"Ugh," said Ruth. "There's more propaganda, or jingo-ism, more would-be public opinion, promoted in one of those songs, than in a dozen speeches by Teddy Roosevelt or the Preparedness folks."

"Well, I'm all for preparedness, but I'd rather not fight just for fun," Mary said. "Grab the next trolley we see. It's getting later, and we're not making enough progress."

Ruth agreed, and they continued across town.

"I've felt the presence of other people watching us; you know: furtive movements to avoid looking me in the eyes, some faces you think you've seen again and again this afternoon; similar to trying not to spook horses you want to catch," explained Ruth. "Hard to put into words until you see it, like the stalking skills for hunting game."

Mary nodded she understood. She noted the Austrian beer hall across the street, and realized they'd strayed.

"Shadowed, we learn we are worth noticing in some bigger game. It might be a clue, or a connection to our missing man. A small, not very happy success."

"Hmm," said Ruth. "If British agents watch the major Irish and German social groups, they may have seen us buying ads in the 'Gaelic-American' and the 'Volkszeitung'. This British influence may be why the detective dropped our case."

"Uh-huh. A foreign relations issue damaging to British and American ties… You see? They're moving in."

Ruth nodded. "Two more ruffians angling across the street.

Three men dressed as Lascars at the corner ahead. They'll try to stop us, while the main team moves in to seize us."

"And some cars and vans slowing up and stopping," Mary noted. "A big closed sedan edging along the opposite curb, and the electric brougham the driver's just unhooking from the charging station."

"The crowd's vanishing. They feel trouble," hissed Ruth.

"When they charge they'll try to push us into the cars.

"Time to stand back to back. Be ready to draw, that'll make them pause, and then shoot anybody who makes another move," advised Ruth.

"No," said Mary. "It's too early for gunfire, even here on the West Side. Let me make a call."

She raised her face, brightened by the sun low in the West, and loosed a long warbling chortle of song that carried through the neighborhood, yodeling, to the surprise of hundreds on the street and hundreds more watching from open windows, fire escapes, and front stoops in the four- and five-story canyon.

Mary's call rose and fell, almost like speech, as she yodeled the short Western Swiss 'M'aidez!'; clear liquid notes pleading for aid, filling the block, ending in a tone of desperation no man could ignore.

For a moment, all motion, all noise seemed to stop in the street.

The muggers surrounding Mary and Ruth paused, confused, as another yodel, from a male voice, answered, followed by a veritable chorus of men shouting, yodeling in response.

The doors of the beer hall gave way to a tumbling wave of sailor-men pouring down the steps, filling the sidewalk, curb, and out to the streetcar tracks.

The excited men jostled, shouted, "Sehen Sie?," "See, that?," "Yo, ho!," "Wir comen!"

Rough men, too long ashore and idle, looking for a challenge, or better, a fight, any diversion, their best uniforms reduced to well-patched, threadbare, little better than rags, but mended with pride and untiring industry.

All this the crowd of threatening bravos recognized in a moment.

Three dozen men swarmed out of the brightly-lit doorway of the Oester-reich Hofbrauhaus. Their eyes flashed at the prospect of a good fight as they saw two young women standing back-to-back in a circle of threatening figures.

As forty noisy sailors surged forward, many in the crowd, including the assailants, recalled an urgent appointment across town, somebody who owed them money, or a necessary function best performed anywhere else, and scrambled away with more haste than concern for image.

To Ruth's amazed glance, Mary said, "I've been listening and practicing with the cowboys in Kansas."

"The sailors from the Tyrolean place, they're waving. Let's wave back," recommended Ruth.

Jarst and his officers came down from the steps, keeping an eye on their men.

"I think this is what we call a Mexican stand-off," pronounced the first uniformed policeman to arrive, as he viewed the two young women standing safely within the double ranks of sailors and stokers formed up at a command from their bos'n, and facing outward.

Mary and Ruth stepped up and presented their New York City permits for the officer, who smiled at them and scowled fiercely at the neighborhood rubber-neckers gathered for the spectacle. More of them drifted back into the deep shadows of the coming evening.

Two New York Policemen on horseback trotted briskly around to study the crowd for instigators to riot, or any criminals known to them, and the crowd dispersed rapidly. The suspicious cars earlier had vanished around corners.

A uniformed police captain and a beat cop briefly asked questions, looked over the sailors returning to the bar, and were called away to deal with a bomb threat at an Italian grocery two blocks up, and a robbery call closer to the waterfront. The Paddy Wagon rattled away empty. A typical Friday night forming up for the police.

A gentleman in a good, if slightly out-of-style, suit stepped up and made a courtly Old World bow. Mary noticed the hazel eyes of a man of medium height and age showing friendly confidence, who could hold onto his hat when the emergency sounded.

"Dargo Jarst, Chief Engineer of Steamship 'Martha Washington'," the gentleman said. "At your service, ladies. My shipmates, Rudy Bregenz, Third Deck Officer, and Urfan Groljnik, Purser." They also bowed, showing winning smiles.

Jarst bowed again to present his card, embossed with Imperial and Royal Austria's double eagle, the name of his ship, and the company, Vereinigte oesterreichische Schiffahrtsgesellshaften der Austro-Americana und der Gebrueder Cosulich, and his own name and position.

Mary couldn't help blushing when introducing Ruth and herself, and gave Jarst her calling card, which he read aloud:

Mary Bodacia Cowles

"Bodacia, after the Rebel Queen of Ancient Britain?" and he bowed again.

"Ruth Cowles, Peoples' Line Excursions," he said, reading Ruth's card, and looked at both of them.

"That could explain what's going on here," and he indicated the idlers and rubber-neckers being made to feel too conspicuous by a couple of blue-coated New York policemen walking calmly about.

"Perhaps a robbery attempt. Someone may have fingered you as carrying large amounts of cash for your company.

"I, too, am a reader of the 'National Police Gazette', Miss Cowles.

"It was Rudy here who identified your timely call for aid, and Groljnik called the police. Our deck crew and firemen at the bar were the first to respond to your distress call.

"I think they saved you ladies from being shanghaied, so I'm standing them drinks to celebrate our victory, even if it was your Mexican stand-off."

Jarst motioned toward the 'Oesterreich' behind him.

"Will you ladies join us at a table in our restaurant; it's not a saloon, I assure you," Jarst said, indicating the 'Oesterreich' behind him.

"Oyster-wreck?" asked Ruth, still a little jumpy.

"Eastern Realm," explained Jarst, as Mary frowned slightly and nudged Ruth.

"We'll be delighted to join you, Mein Herr. I must make a telephone call to Electric Livery Cab."

Inside, Jarst summoned waiters to bring extra chairs to his officers' table, and invited Mary and Ruth to dine with them, and the ladies, after a momentary glance to confer with each other, accepted with thanks.

Jarst ordered tall glasses of 'Usk-wasser' beer for his officers, "and for you ladies?"

"Two Cel-Ray Sodas by Doctor Brown," finished Mary. "We are tee-totallers, total abstainers in our First Christian Church."

"Old Preacher LaRue also warned against gambling, dancing, and excessive levity; or you might otherwise find us in fan-tan parlors in China Town, or idling away our afternoons with the Tango pirates on Fifth Avenue," said Ruth. "We'll be serving aboard the Peoples' Line 'C.W. Morse' as Purser and Cashier for the summer excursions up the River."

"Oh, yes, of course. Over here at Pier 32," said Bregenz.

Ruth and Mary made a brief summary of their efforts to locate their sister's missing husband, and the alarming developments of the last few days.

"Police, gangsters, and maybe spies; they're showing too much interest, where we expected public indifference to our missing man inquiries. Could there be larger issues involved?"

Jarst made vague remarks, intending for comfort, echoed by his officers, speculating that the scramble for wartime profits must be unsettling for all levels of such a large, crowded metropolis, teeming with people grasping for success; and with what he hoped were not political or leading comments, gave his best professional smile, no less real for being a commercial property. As always, the ladies were quite distracted by his smile.

Privately, he recognized that these women had crossed tracks with trouble, and it was obvious he must get shed of these unlucky Americans to protect his own secrets. He always enjoyed such company as these petite blondes, with dimples when they smile, my goodness, but they seem to have attracted the attention of dangerous, powerful persons. Best cut them adrift, with haste.

"I understand that the new 'Foxtrot' dance is a white musician arrangement from 'Ragtime'," suggested Groljnik. "And there's that new sound…No, not the 'Blues'. Something else from the Delta… Improvisational, jagged. I'll know it when I hear it again."

"We may be able to hire some African bands for our concerts and dances aboard the boats this summer. We know their Union representatives," offered Mary.

Groljnik and Bregenz exchanged glances as the same thought occurred to them.

"May we send our ship's band leader to call at your office, Miss Cowles? Our liner's band is too often idle, even here in this great port, and might contribute as alternate, or filling-in musicians for your vessel."

Ruth gave each of them her business card with office telephone numbers, and her sincere thanks for their providential intervention.

"You might also approach the Musician's Local 310 and One-Twenty-Three about membership for your band members. Mention my name. I've heard them complain about the marooned German and Austrian bandsmen picking up local gigs," advised Ruth.

Mary and Ruth ordered the Wiener schnitzel breaded veal, with lettuce and vinaigrette dressing, and potatoes in butter and chive sauce, and weren't surprised when the Austrian officers ordered baked salmon and roast potatoes, (Friday, Mary figured) young carrots and turnips garnished with Italian herbs. Over savory food, conversation dealt with experiences, homes, and families.

"The carnival we hold just before Lenten season in my home port of Rijeka; I've enjoyed it since childhood. All the costumes, music, dancing; parties throughout the city in every street and neighborhood."

"The rule of Saturn, you know, when everything was better," quoted Jarst. He went on to outline his education at the Austro-Hungarian Naval Academy in Rijeka, on the plateau above the Adriatic Sea, "always as blue as the eyes of the wife of Neptune, the Sea-God."

Travels with the Imperial and Royal Navy, and his move to commercial shipping, ending with advancement to maintaining the passenger liner 'Martha Washington' between Europe and America, Jarst hastened to summarize.

The third mate, Rudy, told a wry anecdote about his Great-Uncle, now Bishop of Zwischen-Wasser, "in Feldkirch, you know," and his medical work and preaching of Christianity among New Guinea tribes, some of whom... "Well, they still think of him as their brother-in-law."

Groljnik related legends of his clan sweeping down from the high country to fight Venetians and Turks, under the banner of a hero whose name was unfamiliar to Ruth and Mary. Groljnik wanted to hear more about the stern old patriarch who founded a new Church in America.

"A pioneer in the Campbell-Stone movement, for the unity of Christianity; I never met him;" said Ruth, smiling (to her surprise), "He was my grandfather's generation, and was killed by Indians on Bear Creek, Kentucky, or else by bears at Indian Creek; I can't recall which."

The image in Groljnik's mind, of a bemused bear watching a European and an Indian fighting, or, of a bear chasing a bearded preacher along a shallow creek bed while two Indians stand and point, threw Groljnik into violent laughter, to the concern of his companions.

Mary restrained herself from correcting Ruth; it was John Morgan LaRue with the Indians, in 1780.

Fascinated by the officers describing life in the combined Empire and Kingdom of Austria-Hungary, Mary and Ruth came to understand it was a recent invention during the reign of Emperor Franz Josef, rather than an ancient entity. Mary thought of the many nationalist movements, and attempts to split off the several Slavic identities into new Balkan states, the source of this new War that had overcome Europe.

Oceans, commerce with foreign climes, and historic lands caught Mary in particular, and it was with real regret she heard the talk turn inevitably from personal adventures in the China Seas or steaming through the glorious splendors of the warm Mediterranean, to the current tragedy of the War.

"This cruiser of the French Navy, 'Descartes' is..."

"Oh, I know! 'I sink, therefore I am'," Ruth, too, tried to keep a light tone to the conversation, and made no apology for her interruption, since she was rewarded with smiles.

"As I was saying," and Jarst smiled wider. "The cruiser stops American vessels of the New York and Porto Rico Line, carrying mail and passengers, in order to search for German citizens; took four German-born firemen out of the boiler-room on 'S.S. Coumo', the chief steward off 'S.S. Carolina'; and 'S.S. San Juan' lost a couple of German passengers.

"William Jennings Bryan," here Jarst paused as Mary put a hand over her heart for the name she'd always supported, "uh, Your Secretary of State may write France a letter of protest for interfering with the Federal Mail service, and, of course, the passengers between United States ports like New York and Porto Rico.

"Remember, if you'll excuse me for taking a lecturing tone, actions like that led to your Second War with Britain, and almost again when a Union warship removed Confederate government ministers from a British liner," pontificated Jarst, moved to exhibit his knowledge of American history.` Mary reacted with a touch of impatience, "Not as bad as that U-boat sinking the liner 'Falaba' three weeks ago, that drowned a hundred innocent passengers, one of whom was an American."

"I can't defend unrestricted submarine warfare. No justification for killing civilians. It's worse than piracy, to the mind of honest sailors of any nation," Jarst admitted, and looked regretful and abashed. He thought to himself, we're locked to Germany's Kaiser, rather than our own; bound to the whims of a savage, or a child, wielding modern weapons.

"What about the 'S.S. Odenwald' trouble in Puerto Rico?" Ruth figured it was time to sheer off.

The two junior officers automatically deferred to their chief engineer.

"Hamburg-Amerika (which between you and me is almost an arm of the German Government, but you didn't hear it from me) operates 'Dampschiffe Odenwald'," said Jarst, his greater comfort with German and Austrian technical terms instead of their English counterparts suggesting he was just a little distracted. How can blue eyes make me rattle like an over-heated piston ring?

"Uh, anyway, they sheltered her in the neutral United States port of San Juan, and then 'Odenwald' tried to leave San Juan harbor without clearance papers, laden with an unexplained cargo of steamer-grade coal.

"France and Britain allege that the extra coal was to re-supply Germany's 'Kronprinz Wilhelm', an armed ship operating as a commerce raider."

Remember incidents of bunkering, thought Jarst, one of the dirtiest, most dangerous tasks around ships, even in sheltered havens; then think of shifting coal on the open sea, and the horrendous accidents when ships must deal with each other on the wide, hostile ocean.

A waiter approached, announcing, "A car for Miss Cowles," and Jarst and his officers rose.

Outside, the Austrians made references to their pleasure at the introductions, and various assurances of their services, always at the call of the Misses Cowles.

"Auf wiedersehen," Jarst said, and wished them "a summer of happy voyaging," gaining the Austrians more thanks and warming smiles. The officers saluted, and bowed the ladies into their tall, all-windowed cab.

As they departed, Jarst wondered if he should revise his assessment. The Cowles sisters seemed self-reliant, and remarkably well-informed on current events. Were they more active players in the New York intrigues than they appeared?

All these intelligence operatives, spies, counter-spies, informants, assassins! Too many to watch, and his supposed allies, the Germans were plotting against each other, even in the presence of their enemies, petty intrigues too foolish for melodrama and music-hall comedy, thinking it suitable for wartime strategy.

Best thing, Jarst decided, 'Don't under-estimate the Americans.'

* * *

Waiting for sleep in his waterfront garret, Raff considered his next moves.

He'd thought of buying an automobile. A guy in Brooklyn who would sell him a nice flashy Reo Runabout, not too old, for the gold Raff got from the railroad man. Maybe some other time.

He recalled how, after his last errands of the day, he had wandered into the Downtown office of the N.A.A.C.P., passing under the dark banner that announced:

> ## A MAN WAS LYNCHED YESTERDAY

Seemed to Raff, that banner flew more often than the Stars and Stripes flew at half-mast for a dead Senator, or an old Civil War hero, and some things needed to be supported, so he didn't mind dropping a purse of gold British sovereigns on the receptionist's desk, to bring his membership up to date.

The young woman who typed sat there as upon a throne, and showed no surprise, but made out a receipt, and called the office manager, who shook Raff's hand.

Then he remembered his Lodge brothers in the Royal Society of Oddfellows who could tell him how to get started in law. Or maybe the NAACP folks could advise. Must be a law school around New York, wouldn't you think?

Why did that young woman make him think of jaguar skins, tropical birds, and elephants?

* * *

A fast, quiet trip in Electric Livery Cab, and within their safe refuge:

"Mary, this passenger list for the Ward Line's steamship 'Monterey' shows William Haines of Kansas City on the Thursday, April first voyage to Havana. That would get him to Havana in time for the big fight," said Ruth. "And he bought a ticket in Manhattan for a return trip on the 'Morro Castle'."

"Something's wrong there," Ruth continued. "We checked all the ships of United Fruit, New York and Cuba Mail Steamship, Mallory Lines, even the small firms; as well as the Dutch, French, and British lines calling there. No trace of him on any returning voyage. What are we missing?"

Mary stood up from her bed, upon which she'd been lounging, struck now by a surprising thought.

"What day was April the First?"

"Thursday."

"It was also April Fool's Day," said Mary in a quiet voice.

"Did Mister Haines leave a nasty message for Nova, or did somebody else buy a ticket on that day to cover his tracks? Could Mister Haines have been a courier for revolutionary monies, or just used as a decoy to draw off spies and robbers from the real courier?"

They both looked at the wall map of the Eastern Seaboard, and at the vast blue void between New York City and Cuba.

Mournful calls of boat horns sounded to Mary like lost souls crossing the River.

She shivered.

Somewhere in the quiet house a telephone jangled, again, and once more before it was answered.

In a few moments came a knock at their door.

CHAPTER TWELVE
Interview With The Monopoly Man

"This is Ruth Cowles…"

Both young women huddled nervously in the hall by the telephone, where Mrs. Markowitz had summoned them for a call. Mary noted the bilious green wallpaper, decorated with leaves and vague flower-like shapes, around the staircase, and around the entrance hallway. Thin, but easily cleaned with soap and rags if anyone brushed dirt on it.

"Yes, ma'am, she is, would you like to…yes, ma'am… I see…we will, yes, ma'am…she's hung up," Ruth exclaimed, looking at Mary. "That's Mrs. Palk, secretary for Uncle Charles' household. I met her last week, she's new, and all business. She'll call us first thing in the morning at our office."

"What does this mean, Ruth?"

"Uncle Charles requires our presence at noon. Mrs. Palk says we stepped on some toes, and people are calling Uncle Charles to account. He will explain our new duties and assignments," said Ruth.

"Well, then, it sounds like we still have employment here," commented Mary, with some relief. "Maybe we'll even get word of Mister Haines."

Ruth gave a skeptical shrug.

During a long restless night at the boarding house, Ruth and Mary discussed the events and encounters of the past few days and tried to make sense of it all. As dawn approached, they found time to wash, and changed to fresher clothes, and crept out as the sun came up, caught a trolley, then transferred to the line that brought them past their waterfront office.

"We would have called on Aunt Clem and Uncle Charles this week, anyway, after we had the excursion schedule in hand," said Ruth, as they peeled some oranges and bananas for breakfast, and heated some water for coffee.

At the hour of opening their office, the telephone rang. Ruth grabbed it.

"Peoples' Line Excursions, this is... yes, ma'am, we're ready... I'm writing it down... yes, ma'am...she's hung up," said Ruth.

The bustle of the pier traffic and the work of mechanics and engineers fitting out the big side-wheel excursion steamer with electric hoists,noisy air tools, and shouted orders kept the sisters too distracted to worry much, and they wrote out and typed programs and schedules to promote the summer River rides.

At 11:20 AM, after a long morning occupied by pointless shuffling of business forms, and checking over boxes of souvenir postcards showing the excursion boats and Hudson River scenery, pamphlets and maps to be sold to ships' passengers, a large, black chauffeured Locomobile pulled into the yard in front of the Excursion Company office, and honked a trumpet twice.

A woman with a long pale spring coat over her business dress and jacket descended from the machine, and held up a large card marked with the letters "R" and "M", whereupon Ruth nodded to Mary, and they took their coats and hats and stepped out. Ruth locked the front door, and they sat down in the back seat with Mrs. Palk, who gave them "Good morning," a thin smile from somewhere in early middle age and said to the driver: "Woolworth Building, Broadway entrance." The car pulled out onto Eleventh to head Downtown.

"Mister Morse will see you in his new office on the Eighty-sixth Floor," said Mrs. Palk.

Mary thought about that. 86th floor? After the Eiffel Tower, Woolworth is the tallest building in the world, but still only 750 feet tall. Hmm. Maybe number from a sub-cellar, the footings go down another hundred feet to bedrock.

As though reading her mind, Mrs. Palk explained.

"Observation Deck. The fifty-five levels of the Woolworth Building are each higher than standard office stories."

The limousine pulled to a stop in front of 233 Broadway; the neo-Gothic tower rising out of sight. Mary noted details of the terra-cotta panels glazed to look like limestone. The chauffeur held the car door, and they followed the secretary through shining bronze and crystal doors, down wide stairs along balustrades of Skyros marble from Greece, swirling with light and dark, polished to gleam.

Down into an arcade and lobby, arranged in a cruciform shape, ceilings curved in lofty domes and barrel-like vaults, brilliant with gold leaf and well-rubbed bronze, and adorned with lines of ornate stone sculpture and decorations depicting friends of Frank Woolworth, including Gilbert the architect and the engineers and builders of this 'Cathedral of Commerce'.

Light flashing from stained glass windows, and a splendor of multi-colored mosaics in Byzantine and Oriental styles, glowing tiles in rainbow colors, dazzled the eyes of the visitors.

Vaguely in passing, Mary noted some of the tenants listed on the boards in the lobby, like Irving Trust Bank, Columbia Records, Professor Tesla, Fordham University, as well as several foreign consulate offices.

"His private elevator. Automatic," announced Mrs. Palk, directing them in as the beaten bronze doors slid aside, but staying outside herself.

So fast, thought Mary, what's that pressure in my ears, and here we are!

Hardly time to catch their balance as the elevator car stopped and compressed air hissed to open the door, revealing a spacious plaza lit briefly by the sunlight, alternately bright, then shaded by the racing clouds.

A black silk hat and a simple cane of silver-mounted ebony rested on a side table, as though their owner had just arrived, and he rose from behind a small curved desk of maple to greet them with a smile.

Charles Morse wore a fine-tailored, but plain black suit, which set off his round, short figure and complemented his white hair, wide white moustache, and pointed white Van Dyke beard.

"Mary, Ruth," he said, stepping forward, "pleased to see you again, and safe. Time presses. Allow me to speak as your Dutch uncle.

"In Town less than a week, Mary, and your investigations and prying have disturbed the uneasy balance of Great Powers, who work mostly unseen, the hidden gang struggles, and Police Department efforts in New York City.

"Shipping and rail stocks have stumbled, there are threats of labor strikes and race riots among the dock workers, there's a new Tong war."

"You innocently tripped over hidden strings stretching all over Manhattan, alerted secret services, revolutionaries; exposed plots and counter-plots, most carefully concealed, some by enemies, and plans of friends and allies.

"Somehow, you intercepted a message from a Japanese faction friendly to our Naval Intelligence; you've been code-named 'the Kaiser's Butterfly'," Charles Morse held up a hand at Mary's gasp. "It's not your fault, I know; information is a reasonable goal, same as money and influence here."

"Last night I received many irate visitors and angry 'phone calls when some of these people found out the Cowles Sisters are my shirt-tail relations, as well as employees. They expect me to chastise you and rein you in, before their unhappiness upsets the City."

"I owe my British friends much for their help obtaining my pardon from Federal prison, where I might still be enjoying Signor Ponzi's company.

"I'll do everything to support the War Supplies Purchasing Commission. For example," and he waved his hand at the large, open room with the unmatched view, "I rented the top of this building, rather than let the Germans occupy it, when they bid on it.

"I help the British efforts as I set up another holding company, my specialty, for sea-going vessels from any source, gathering as much tonnage as I can, with my government's and bank's approval. Another chance for me as a monopoly man. And for you."

"All my employees are receiving bonuses of blocks of stock in this company, and for each voyage, dividends of one hundred percent may be expected. We'll all profit, immensely.

"But I require more from each of you. To calm the shattered nerves of my secretive friends, you both must be less noticeable. Ruth, you will continue to work the Summer excursions, and stay in safety at your Aunt Clem's and my home Uptown, when not on the water.

"But you, dear Mary, must get out of Town. Today. This afternoon. It will be seen as punishment, dismissal, at the insistence of the British and American intelligence organizations, and I think, to the relief of President Wilson's government.

"Don't feel crushed; I'm sending you on an all-expenses-paid trip West, to attend the Expositions in California, where you will draw the troubled thoughts of our jittery and powerful neighbors to the Land of the Lotus-Eaters, so we may all get back to acquiring scandalous piles of wealth supporting Europe's War."

A happy smile showed between his moustache and Van Dyke.

Uncle Charles led the ladies to the great windows overlooking the City, the Rivers and the Bay. Under a spring sky filled with chasing clouds, New York still glittered with riches and vibrated with unrestrained human vigor.

"Some enemy schemes we know, and cherish for the right time to expose their wickedness; other plots we still seek to comprehend."

"Even more embarrassing: the intrigues of our friends and allies, which must be protected, even if only for those peoples' reputations."

"So much to observe, consider, and not speak of, but act upon." He pointed South.

"Oh, look, down the Bay, the 'Lusitania' is standing out to sea."

Uncle Charles consulted a heavy pocket watch.

"Two hours late. You've seen her photos. So large a ship, if you stood her on end Downtown, her prow would be level with us here among New York's tallest skyscrapers.

"Now, look over to the East, past the bridges, where the Brooklyn Navy Yard prepares to launch our new Battleship 'Arizona'."

The elevator door hissed open.

"Here is your Aunt Clem, and our secretary to escort you to your train," he blew a kiss to his wife, dressed in a simple gray and blue town outfit, who always reminded Mary of the statuesque Lillian Russell.

Charles Morse smiled.

"Be sure to view the Grand Canyon, Mary."

* * *

"School will mail my last paycheck here. I'll send you a forwarding address," said Mary after sisterly farewells were made, not without tears. She had hardly noticed the ride up to Pennsylvania Station, nor saw the gray granite facade of the station on Thirty-third Street.

Clutching her traveling clothes, parasol, and handbag, (with three thick envelopes of money). Everything else would ship out next express.

Ruth slipped a few small items into her sister's hands, and finally a folded postcard of the Woolworth Building, with one word penciled on it: 'Decoy'. Mary understood the warning, and nodded.

Shoot! Kicked out of New York City! Mary resigned herself to leaving Manhattan, that great Vessel forever steaming from the land of the Material, towards the Ocean of Possibilities, and realized her life might be taking a new course.

She left the City, walking down an arcade of warm, light-colored stone, passing into a great open birdcage of tall steel girders, to descend to the underworld of dark tunnels, tracks, and waiting trains.

Many eyes noted her leaving. One pair followed close behind.

Post Card

"Broadway Limited" Passing Altoona

Ruth!
Someone followed me
aboard the "Limited,"
I'm sure I shan't
sleep! Mary

End of 'WEST OF WAR'

Follow Mary in 'West To Joy', coming soon.

Notes

1. Mary Beda Cowles (188? - 1938) born and raised on her family's Missouri farm between the towns of Auxvasse and Mexico. Attending high school, she also took summer classes at Christian University in Canton, Missouri, and taught at Skull Lick, Sunrise, Star and other one-room rural schools. Graduating, she found higher-paying school positions in Kansas, joining her sister Ruth at her summer job on New York's Hudson River.

2. Ruth Cowles (1890-1989) born and raised on her family's farm in Calloway County, Missouri between the towns of Auxvasse and Mexico. She heeded the call of the Big City, but went East, instead of to Kansas City, like her sister Nova. Her aunt Clem helped get her a job as Purser aboard the 'C.W. Morse' steamer on the Hudson River summer seasons.

3. Charles Wyman Morse (1856 – 1933) cornered the market in ice during the hottest summer ever in New York City, and made a pile. Put it into shipping, hoping to make it big like J.P. Morgan. He and his friend Heintzie tried to corner the market in copper, ruined some banks, and started the Panic of 1907. Convicted of bank naughtiness, Morse went to Federal prison in Atlanta, where his cell-mate was Carlo Ponzi. Influential friends won Morse a Presidential pardon right away, and he went back to frolic in the shipping industry. His images in photos, plus his biography, suggest he may have been the model for the Monopoly Man™.

4. 'C.W. Morse' (1904-1934) sidewheel paddle steamer built for People's Line overnight excursions, New York City – Albany. 430' long, 50' beam, 9' draft, steel hull, wooden up`pers, 30' diameter wheels driven by 4500 horsepower walking-beam engine, maximum speed 17 knots. Crew: fifty, steward's department: 25, plus 52 waiters. Passengers up to 900, plus freight, and private autos. 1917-1919, served as receiving ship for U.S. Navy for World War One. Named for Charles Wyman Morse.

5. Hugo Gernsback (1884-1967) born in Luxembourg, immigrated to U.S. With parents. Started a mail-order serve for electrical and radio parts, publishing a catalogue, adding scientific articles, and fiction, re-naming what was now a magazine, 'Electrical Experimenter'. His line of magazines featured science fiction, or 'Scientifiction' as he first called it.

6. Sidney Reilly (1874-1925) probably born in Odessa, Crimea, Russia as Zigmund or Schlomo or Georgi Rosenblum. Arrested in 1892 by Tsarist Okhrana Secret Police. Working for William Melville of Scotland Yard in London, England by 1896 as translator. Double agent for Britain and Japan, before and during Russo-Jaspanse War of 1904. Agent for Britain in securing strategic oil concessions in 1906. Spying in German weapons factories later. In New York City 1914-1915 selling armaments and munitions to Russians and Germans.

7. Alexander Nuber von Pereked (1877-1948) Consul-General for the Dual Monarchy of Austria and Hungary, at 24 State Street in Manhattan. Spies and agents worked out of his office, but they didn't all work for him and his Monarch.

8. Theda Bara (1885-1955) born Theodosia Goodman in Cincinnati, Ohio. 'The Vamp'. While acting in New York theaters, appeared as extra in locally produced Fox movies. Noticed by director Frank Powell, she starred in his film of Porter Emerson Browne's play, 'A Fool There Was', and achieved instant fame in 1915, making several other hit movies that year.
See 'Vamp: The Rise and Fall of Theda Bara', by Eve Golden, published 1998.

9. Lori Bara (1903-1965) born Esther Goodman in Cincinnati, Ohio. Younger sister of Theda, wrote for the movies, and appeared in many, including '7 Chances', with Buster Keaton

10. Simon Lake (1866-1945) Using experiences of working in his father's foundry, he built a working submarine 'Argonaut, Jr.'in 1894, then 'Argonaut I' in 1898, traveling a thousand miles in it, winning kudos from Jules Verne. Lake designed 'Protector', included several innovations, such as a lock for working divers, but U.S. Navy turned it down, Lake's next submarines went to Russia, Austria-Hungary, and Germany.'

Successes noted by U.S. Navy, for whom Lake built USS G-1, which set depth record of 256 feet for Navy in 1913. Lake developed commercial salvage equipment of great value, but was distracted by naval uses of submarines.

11. Vahan Cardashian (1883-1934) born at Gesaria, he immigrated from Turkey in 1902, graduated from Yale Law, and set up practice in New York City, where he served as Consul for the Ottoman Empire in 1915, organizing exhibits at the Panama-Pacific Exposition in San Francisco.

12. Aleister Crowley (1875-1947) writer, mountaineer, sorcerer, major influence on New Age religions in the Twentieth Century. Calling Magick a practical art to be developed, he founded Ordo Templi Orientis, and Thelema. In New York City in 1915, writing for magazines, the editor of 'The Fatherland' (pro-German) actually paid him for articles in which Crowley mocked the Kaiser, using subtle sarcasm. Traveling West in 1915 to speak in Saint Paul and Detroit and inspecting pharmaceutical companies for hallucinogenic drug processes, he also may have spied on German sympathizers on the West Coast.

13. David Lamar (1877-1934) Wall Street operator, gangster, con man. Assisted German agents like von Rintelen to buy influence and munitions, assist with bribes to newspapers and unions.

14. Franz von Rintelen (1877-1949) arrived in New York City on April 3rd, 1915 under a false name and passport, assigned to sabotage or otherwise interrupt munitions shipments from America to the British and their allies. A Naval Intelligence officer from Germany, he worked independently, causing alarm, jealousy and resentment in Germany's diplomatic staff in America, like Ambassador Bernstorff, Naval Attaché Karl Boy-Ed, and Paul Koenig of Hamburg-Amerika Shipping Lines. He set up a huge bank account for propaganda, labor strikes, and sabotage in New York's Transatlantic Trust Company, and organized a fake purchasing company to buy up, horde, destroy, or otherwise remove from availability all explosives, machine tools, and chemicals used in producing munitions.

15.   Doktor Heinrich Albert (1874-1960) Commercial attaché to United States for Germany, a career bureaucrat back home, he was actually paymaster for all the propaganda, spying, and dirty tricks. He really did let go of his briefcase full of papers and letters that exposed Germany's hostility toward America's support for Britain and the Allies, and all the illegal acts German agents could commit against the neutral United States, its ports, shipping, and industries. The damaging letters found their way to American officials raising more than a few eyebrows, causing alarm, and leading to severe counter-espionage.

Most histories credit U.S. Secret Service people, or other American police with the actual snatch of the briefcase, but the Czech patriot, Emanuel Voska (1875-1960) wrote in his 1940 book, 'Spy and Counter-spy', that his Czech co-workers, wanting freedom from Austria-Hungary for their home, plotted and accomplished this theft. Did the Americans take the credit in 1915 to keep secret the Czech moles in the Austrian consulate? The involvement of Aleister Crowley has been suggested by Richard Spence in his recent book, 'Secret Agent 666'; Aleister Crowley, British Intelligence, and the Occult'. We now know the identity of the woman on the Elevated, who tried to prevent the theft.

16. Son of a Civil War hero, Anton Dilger (1889-1918?), native born American citizen, a fanatic supporter of Germany, served as battlefield surgeon in a Balkan war and for German forces on the Western Front in the Great War. Wanting to strike back at American industry that supported Britain and France and manufactured weapons killing Germans, he volunteered to Captain Nadolny of the Abteilung to carry disease cultures of Anthrax and Glanders lethal to stock animals and human beings, and to spread them where the diseases would most hurt America.

See 'The Fourth Horseman: The Tragedy of Anton Dilger and the Birth of Biological Terrorism', by Robert Koenig, published, 2007.

His plans, often requiring help from hired dupes, fizzled out without obvious effect. One of his minions was Brooklyn-born Frederic Herrman. Maybe prompt action by people close-by broke the plot and frightened him out of the country?

About the Author

John Hartigan Waldo is a Journeyman Blacksmith.
Other volumes include science fiction, blacksmith instruction, as well as other works of historical fiction.

https://thekaisersbutterfly.wordpress.com/